Stories of women's Magic Over Men

Joel Willans

First published by Route in 2012
PO Box 167, Pontefract, WF8 4WW
info@route-online.com
www.route-online.com

ISBN: 978-1901927-56-6

Joel Willans asserts his moral right to be
identified as the author of this book

Design:
GOLDEN
www.wearegolden.co.uk

Printed and bound by CPI Group (UK) Ltd, Croydon, CR0 4YY

A catalogue for this book is available from the British Library

Route is supported by Arts Council England

For Anna Maria

Stories

One Bright Moment

We were children, not lovers, but as we lay on the grass, staring at stars, she took my hand and said that a moment can change everything. When I think of Sissy Zaleski, and I do now more often than ever, I always remember her that night. Splayed out on the earth as though floating just an inch above the ground, she told me in the strange quiet of the countryside, where silence is made up of infinite little sounds, that there would be signs, forever.

'I'm not tricking you. You know that, don't you? I'm just telling you how it is and how it's going to be. When we get older and we're not friends 'cause we've gone away or got a job or got married, I'm going to send you signs to remember us now, this very second. Do you believe me?'

'What sort of signs?'

She was about to answer when the lamplight came through the leaves, but I was already on my feet, tugging her up, dragging and scrambling with her hand tight in mine, keeping low to the ground as the lamplight swept to and fro, a hulking shadow stomping behind it.

'Sissy, you better not be out here with that boy! You hear me?'

Even now I can see her dad. A stomper, always a stomper, with dark eyes and a darker brow. And always dangerous, with tools in bulging pockets. That time he stomped the earth, and we rushed into the night. In the trees, near the stream, we stopped and sat on our haunches, breathing hard, breathing the woods. We stayed liked that, frozen in our fear, until I moved closer and whispered in her ear:

'Why does he hate me so much? I ain't done anything wrong.'

She moved closer still. 'He thinks if it weren't for you, I'd stay indoors more with him. Now Mum's left.'

I looked into her eyes. Then, like idiots feeling safe and holding nothing back, we hugged together, so close I could feel her heart next to mine. I don't know who kissed whom first. But once, years later, in a room in Blackpool, watching as my wife combed her hair, ochre red like Sissy's, it came to me with force as crushing as gravity. If I'd kept Sissy closer, if I'd never let her go so easy, it could have been her combing herself in front of me then. I wonder now if that was the first sign, or if they'd been there all those years and I'd just blanked them out, pressed them down, scared of what they said.

I've had no worse parting than that night. I didn't want her to go, but once we finished, and we realised what we'd done and how now I was more, much more than a forbidden friend, she was shaking so hard I thought she might die on me. With the taste of her on my lips, I sneaked us out of the trees. We scurried close to the ground, as fast as we could, and I took her back to her dad's lair. I kissed her again, in the shadows. It was the bravest thing I'd ever done. I wanted to show her that even though she was going back, I wouldn't desert her. Not ever.

She didn't come to school for a few days after that and then I found out it was she who was leaving me. Going back to Poland, that's what my friend said, to the motherland of her ancestors, as far as the stars for me. I didn't believe him at first, how could I? Since that night, she'd been in every one of my thoughts, colouring them like ink spilled in water. But then they announced it at school, last thing in assembly, after the morning prayers. And when everyone else filed out, I just sat there. Cross-legged and dazed.

I saw her once afterwards. She sneaked round to my house; she couldn't stay long, she said. She threw herself onto the sofa and started wrestling cushions, banging her fists and asking me that if there was a God, then what was he doing to make her dad so mad to leave? I wanted to say things to make her feel better but I couldn't, because I knew that it was me who'd caused it. I wanted to kiss her again too, but my mum was lurking, so I just held her hand and said I'd write every day.

10

Look out for the signs, she said before she left. Little things, I'll send them and you'll remember me. I know it.

And I did to start with. I looked out all the time, but as I changed from boy to man I stopped searching or maybe I just stopped seeing. Life clouding things over.

So why is it only now that my life is drowsy with dreams of her? And what does it mean that a smell, a word, the single sigh of an owl can make me think of Sissy? Nearly a whole life I've lived without her, got jobs, gone away and been married, but only now do I see that she was right. That one moment, one bright culmination of everything, can change you from children to lovers and that you can never, ever, go back again.

Shoot Yourself Dead

I'm in the Spotted Horse, a year to the day that I did a John Wayne and told Natalie a man's got to do what a man's got to do. Why here, in a nicotine-stained pub with ripped tartan bar stools and trill fruit machines? Not to celebrate, but to stare at the No Children Allowed sign and provoke my muse. And, I hope, to finally purge myself of the self-pity which has been hanging off me like a wretched suit. This place was an oasis once, now it's just another grimy drinking den. Still, after a couple of pints, it does its job. I grab my pen and begin writing notes for the main feature of the September issue of *Sorted*.

A dumb name for a dumb magazine. That was the first thing Natalie and I agreed upon. Like a kid trying to work out my age, I count on my fingers. It's nearly three years since we met. Zanadoo Publishing's Christmas Ball, me shooting pistols on the dance floor to Fatboy Slim, Natalie spying me from beneath her black fringe and shooting back. Afterwards she'd sauntered over, wearing the fulsome grin that I later knew meant mischief, and checked out my nametag.

'Hello, Henry Jones,' she said in mock posh tones. 'I'm in sales. What do you do?'

'I have the great privilege of working as a journalist and film critic on the esteemed gentleman's monthly, *Sorted*,' I replied in an accent that would've put the Queen to shame.

When Natalie laughed, she clenched her fists and rocked on her heels, and I noticed she had the most outrageously beautiful neck. By 2am, I was kissing it. Seven months later, we were living together.

I never thought I'd shack up with an ad salesperson. They're too boisterous and brash. Ask any journo who's had to share office space with an ad team and they'll tell you the same. It's like trying to write whilst sitting in the middle of a playground. On a Friday afternoon with a deadline looming, the last thing you want is a football bouncing off your bonce.

On our first date at Natalie's favourite cocktail bar, a cellar with blue neon lights, intimate coves and TV screens above the urinals, I asked her why sales people were so hyperactive. She held up two fingers.

'Rejection and acceptance. If your entire day yo-yoed between those two extremes, you'd regress too. Sales is a game and every month you either win or lose. You think the sales floor is like a playground, because it is a playground.'

'Nothing to do with the copious use of Colombian marching powder, then?'

She laughed. 'Oh, that's just to stop us keeling over with boredom during the breathtakingly dull lunches with marketing managers.'

Her cavalier attitude towards cocaine unnerved me. While I'd always been fond of a drink, I had problems with the white stuff. Not only did it make me spout a monologue called 'Why I'm so fucking great', it also made me less discerning when it came to ladies. One morning, after waking up beside a girl who had so much steel in her face I wondered if she was a human magnet, I decided enough was enough. No matter how great the temptation, or my insecurities, I'd never fire up my brain with charlie again. The ad sales team either didn't share my symptoms or didn't care. Come 5:31pm on any given day, the toilets of Zanadoo Publishing would be busier than Oxford Circus. Still, everyone has their bad habits, and Natalie was too fantastic in other ways for a line or two to get in our way.

I can't say exactly when I realised things were getting serious, but I first told her while watching *Casablanca* at the oldies night at the Odeon. When Humphrey Bogart walked off into the moonlight, I whispered in her ear. 'This may seem like a cheesy moment, but I really want you to know that… well, I love you.'

With the credits rolling, she hugged me closer. 'You know what. That's made my day. Please, say it again, Jonesy.'

And old romantic that I am, I did.

I was thirty-three and I'd fallen in love for the third time. Now, I'm not one for lucky charms or superstition, nor do I know much about numerology, but this trio of threes seemed too much of a coincidence to ignore. Perhaps this was third time lucky, my chance to finally land a lady for life.

We were jogging through Bishop's Park six months after we'd become live-in lovers, when the subject of kids came up. I was gushing over her crossword skills when a couple jogged past, pushing one of those ridiculous three-wheeled buggies that look like mini-dragsters. The thought of Natalie and I accompanied by another tiny jogging partner suddenly filled me with a whisky-warm glow.

'What do you think of that?' I said, nodding in their direction.

'Bloody stupid. That dwarf Tom Cruise might get away with it, but anyone else should be put away for fashion crime.'

'No, not the bizarre pram, but kids.'

She stopped and began jogging on the spot. I did the same. 'Are you asking me what I think of kids in general?'

I nodded. 'Why? Is that a problem?'

'No, as long as it's just asking rather than wanting,' she said and sprinted off. I followed on behind, admiring her rear while wondering what exactly the problem was with a question I considered the epitome of sensitive New Age bloke talk.

I discovered the answer a few weeks later while watching Natalie do her yoga. She'd had to attend one her magazine's award ceremonies the previous evening and was trying to purify her body of any remaining champagne. Sitting cross-legged on the sofa, writing a review of the latest car-chasing-blood-spilling violence porn spewed out of Hollywood, it dawned on me that I had no idea what her favourite film was.

'Hey, Nats, can I ask you a question?' I said as she realigned herself into the sun salutation position, legs spread, arms pointed skyward.

'If you must.'

'What's your favourite movie ever?'

'*Moulin Rouge*,' she said, breathing out through her nose. 'Yours?'

'*The Sound of Music*.'

She dropped to the floor laughing. 'Jesus! Are you serious?'

I nodded. 'It's the third highest grossing film in history for a reason.'

'Hang on. You're the film critic for one of Britain's most laddish magazines. You write features like "How to Assess an Ass" and you're telling me your favourite film is about a singing nun and a bunch of German kids?'

'They were Austrian, and, yes, I am telling you that.'

She slapped the floor, which made her breasts jiggle, which made me want to join her on her yoga mat and invent a brand new position. 'Why, for God's sake?'

I held up two fingers. 'One, I love the tunes.' I started to sing: 'Do, a deer, a female deer. Re, a drop of golden sun. Me, a thing I call myself. Fa, a long, long way to run…'

'Please! I still have a headache.' She held up her hand like a traffic cop. 'I know the tune all right.'

'Two, I'm an only child and when I was a kid I always wanted to have loads of siblings, to be part of a tribe of singing and dancing Joneses. Okay? Is that good enough for you?'

'You have no idea how lucky you were.' She took three deep breaths and exhaled. 'Can you imagine there was much singing and dancing going on with my three brothers and three sisters?'

I shrugged. I'd only met one brother and he seemed like a nice-enough bloke.

'No, there bloody well was not. Ever wondered why I eat so quickly?'

'I always thought you just got hungry easily.'

'That has nothing to do with it. It's an instinct I learnt and can't shake. When I was a kid the dinner table was like a war zone.' She made frantic shoveling-in-your-mouth gestures. 'If I didn't eat my food quick enough it would get snatched off my plate. Every meal time, my mum was like a referee at a rugby match.'

'Ah, so that's why you don't want to be a mother? You're scared.'

She ignored my question, rearranged her body into the next pose and began breathing through her nose like a sleeping Darth Vader. She carried on like that for another half an hour. Finally, with her ying and yang back in balance and her body purged of the evil humours, she clambered back onto the sofa and laid her head in my lap.

'You should have seen my mum before she died. She was fifty-seven, she looked seventy. That's what I'm scared of.'

I stroked her hair. She had the same perfume on as when I'd first nuzzled her neck all those months before. 'I don't want seven kids. I just want one, with you. Think how cool it would be to have someone running around, half you, half me.'

'What, like a centaur?'

I grabbed her face and licked her nose. 'No, not like a bloody centaur. Like a brand new person with my good looks and your incredibly bendy body.'

She smacked me in the face with a cushion. 'Okay, I'll think about it.' I wanted to punch the sky like Rocky after he bounds up a hundred steps. I wanted to run along the beach like those guys in *Chariots of Fire*. I wanted to shake my booty like Tony Manero in *Saturday Night Fever*. Instead, I kissed her forehead and sang, 'Natalie is one of my few favourite things,' only stopping when she whacked me with the cushion again.

Okay, I admit it. I'm something of an obsessive individual. When I was a kid, I would spend hours lining up toy soldiers in phalanxes of a hundred, only so I could destroy their perfect symmetry with a marble bombardment. If I found a particularly fine sentence in a novel I would read it over and over again. When Adam Ant burst onto the music scene, I had to have every single record by the dandy highwayman. My mum blamed my lack of siblings. Another reason why I hoped our one child would become two, maybe even three.

My obsessive nature kicked into gear once Natalie agreed to Project Baby. For a start, sex changed. I'd always prided myself on my Zen-like lovemaking, but now I became more demanding. Sex became my second job. By flooding Natalie's ovaries with my little swimming fellas, I was confident a triumphant declaration of pregnancy would only be a matter of time. It didn't cross my mind that Natalie might be on to me, until one night after a particularly sweaty session, she asked me what I knew about ovulation.

'What do you mean, for women?' I asked, wondering is this was a precursor to the announcement I'd been waiting for.

'No, for elephants. What do you think, Henry?'

'I know you produce eggs every month and they float around in your body. That's about it. Is there anything I'm missing?'

'So you don't know that there are only three days a month when the one egg, singular, can be fertilized?'

'Three days?' I said, thinking that yet another symbolic three cropping up in my life had to be a good sign. 'I had no idea. When are your three days?' I sat up and grabbed a pad from the bedside table.

'Are you writing an article about it?'

'No, I'm just making a note.'

She sighed. 'They began last Wednesday. Does that mean I can only expect such careful attention three times a month now?'

'Don't be stupid,' I said, but as soon as I had a chance I made a note in my diary.

It was during the next month's egg days that we had our first argument. Unsure whether Natalie was doing it out of spite or genuine forgetfulness, I confronted her when she rocked up home late on the first evening of Egg Day One. The way she strutted through the front door at 2.17am, I knew she'd been enjoying more than champagne and cocktails. She flung her coat on the stairs and gave me a sloppy kiss.

'Hello, sailor, what are you doing up still?'

'You know what the date is today?'

'Is this is a quiz?' she giggled.

'No, it's not a fucking quiz.' I grabbed her shoulders and shook her, hard.

'For Christ's sake, Natalie. You know how chilled out I am about you gallivanting around Soho at all hours of the day, but today is an egg day!'

'What on earth are you babbling about?' She wriggled free of my grasp and strolled into the living room.

I steamed after her, feeling anger surge over me. 'Where are you going? Get upstairs and get ready!'

'Get ready for what?'

'For screwing.' Natalie looked at me standing with my arms folded in the doorway. The stench of cigarettes reached my nostrils. 'Have you been smoking as well?'

'Oh, for God's sake, will you listen to yourself. You sound like my dad!'

'It's an egg day!' I shouted. 'And you're getting drunk with your buddies, smoking ciggies and snorting coke like some Hollywood B list brat. What do you think that does to your ovaries?'

'It's Friday!' she screamed. 'I don't think about my ovaries on Fridays! Got it?'

Before I could say anything, she got up, grabbed her coat and wrenched open the front door.

'Where are you going?'

'Back to a place where people treat me like a human being rather than a womb on legs!' She slammed the door shut. As I stood at the window and watched her hailing a taxi, I found myself wondering if her hangover would make her unavailable for the next day, too.

I played it more carefully after that, yet according to the Egg Day Excel spreadsheet I'd created, my sperm met her eggs eighty-seven percent of her most fertile time. I never told her about the spreadsheet or even mentioned egg days again. But Natalie wasn't stupid, she knew that during those three days she could get me to do whatever she wanted. In the following six months, I repainted the kitchen lilac, built her a Japanese rock garden, and joined her doing sun salutations. Although a productive few months, no pregnancy was forthcoming.

It was a spring day and every living thing seemed to be preparing for, having, or caring for babies. We were sitting outside on the terrace of a cafe in Bishop's Park. I'd just bought Natalie a decaffeinated cappuccino and was wondering whether she'd notice, when I popped the question.

'What sort of doctor?' she said, supping her coffee.

I moved closer and whispered. 'A fertility doctor. Just to make sure, you know.'

She screwed her face up. 'God, this coffee tastes rank. To make sure of what?'

'That your lifestyle isn't making it more difficult for us.'

She slammed her mug on the table.

'Are you implying that it's my fault I haven't become pregnant in the last year?'

I reached over and took her hand, surprised that such a sensible suggestion would provoke such a powerful response. If she weren't so immersed in her wine-and-dine, coke-snorting world, she'd see why I was so concerned. She'd see the logic in my proposal.

'I just want to make sure everything is okay? That's all.'

'I presume you'll be getting a sperm test too, then?' she said, throwing her coffee on the grass.

'What?'

'If you want me to spread my legs for some stranger, the least you can do is jerk off into a plastic cup.'

I let go of her hand and leant back in my seat. An old lady on the table next to us was staring at me as if I was something that had just crawled out of the pond. I cracked my knuckles and stretched. John Wayne once said, courage is being scared to death but saddling up anyway. I might not be a cowboy, but if I needed to get my six-shooter out to discover if there was an issue with Natalie, then so be it.

'Let the wagons roll!' I said, downing the rest of my caffeinated coffee.

By the time of our appointment at the London Centre for Reproductive Medicine, my bravado had been replaced by a cocktail of fear, embarrassment and nerves. Our consultant, Doctor Shore, looked like a teenager who'd one day woken up to find herself in a white coat. After firing off questions about our lifestyle and family history, she examined Natalie behind a screen. When they came out, Natalie winked at me.

'Now, Mr Jones, I need your sample. The room is at the end of the corridor. Is fifteen minutes long enough?'

'I suppose,' I said, not wanting to appear awkward.

She handed me a plastic beaker with my name on it.

'Is that big enough?' I asked.

Neither her nor Natalie laughed.

The jerk off room's décor reminded me of an old peoples' home. Beige walls, a print of Van Gogh's 'Sunflowers' and a sink with a pink soap dispenser. I sat on a fake leather chair and turned the TV on. A peroxide blonde was bouncing around on a man with sideburns. I stared at the spectacle for a few minutes, overwhelmed. Like any healthy man, I'd watched porn before, but now the usual sequence of emotions was totally different. Normally, it went from illicit excitement to fulfillment, to self-loathing. On this occasion, I was watching for the benefit of my future family. The most erotic pornography in the world would have been hard pressed to arouse me.

The clock's tick tocking reminded me that this was not the time for philosophising. I cursed Natalie for putting me in this situation and turned the TV off. Then I stood up and yanked my trousers down. With eyes closed, I got to work. What in the right circumstances might take mere seconds, on this occasion seemed like an impossible task. The harder I tried, the less I was forthcoming. Eventually, fearing that someone might knock on the door when my time was up, I flitted through my favourite fantasies until I hit the spot. With a gasp of relief rather than pleasure, I slumped down in the chair. My contribution looked so unimpressive in the beaker that I considered trying again, but the clock said I was out of time.

When I delivered my specimen to the laboratory downstairs, the woman at the counter didn't even say thank you. I tried to appreciate her professionalism, but I couldn't help wonder whether this was simply a huge conspiracy to humiliate men.

I shared this theory with Natalie in the car on the way home and she just laughed. 'I know you're going to hate me for saying this, but sometimes you are just like the men who read your stupid magazine.'

Strangely, the weeks before the results were possibly the best we'd ever had together. I felt happy that Project Baby was moving forward, convinced that now we had medical science on our side, it was only a matter of time before I started my very own Von Trapp family. While Natalie didn't say anything much about the appointment, I caught her singing to herself a few times, and she was especially attentive to my needs. Sunday morning, I was even awoken by a special treat.

'Well, well. What do I owe this pleasure to?' I said, when she nudged me awake and laid a tray of breakfast goodies on my lap.

She shrugged. 'I just felt like being extravagant. Make the most of it. It might just be a phase.'

That evening I spent filming the sunset on my fancy new smartphone. Maybe it was the unseasonably warm weather that filled me with an unusual confidence for the future, but as I panned across the horizon, zooming in and out, I hummed my favourite film theme tunes; *Star Wars, Trainspotting, Doctor Zhivago, The Magnificent Seven.* I was so carried away by these melodies of great moments that I didn't notice Natalie watching me.

'Ready for the doctor's tomorrow?' she said, massaging my shoulders.

'I certainly am. As long as I don't get banished to the jerk off room again.'

'I'll never forget the look on your face when you came back,' she said and sat on my lap. 'But listen, if there's something wrong with me, I'll understand if you want to split up.'

'What! Don't be ridiculous.'

'Seriously. I know how much you've got your heart set on being a daddy and even if sometimes I don't show it, I think it's sweet.' She kissed my forehead.

'Sweet? Don't call me sweet! I write for the country's leading men's magazine. I'll get fired if they hear I'm sweet.'

'Okay, macho man. I just wanted to say.'

After I kissed her back, I played her my mobile film. 'What do you think?'

'David Lynch, eat your heart out,' she said.

But it wasn't Lynch that ate my heart out; it was the good Doctor Shore. The next day at 3.17pm, after she'd told Natalie that she was perfectly okay, she turned to me. I knew immediately from the way she paused something was amiss. She clasped her hands together and looked me straight in the eye.

'I'm afraid there's a problem with your sperm.'

'Sorry?' I said.

She repeated herself and I shook my head, unable to process the consequences of her words. This can't be right. This isn't even about me. The rest of the conversation took place far, far away. In the distance I heard Natalie firing off questions and I heard the phrases 'probably a result of the mumps' and 'no chance of children' and I felt her grip my hand so hard it hurt. But it was all very otherworldly, like the memory of a dream.

It was only when we left and she hugged me on the staircase and I kissed her neck and smelt her favourite perfume that I felt myself back in the now. I tried to think of something to say that was comforting, funny or profound, but nothing came.

'Please don't worry, Henry. It really doesn't matter.'

It did matter of course. Even though Natalie did everything to reassure me that she never even wanted kids, that it was my idea, not hers, I couldn't get the thought out of my head that I'd screwed everything up. She spent the week researching other options, showing me websites and brochures, talking about adoption and fantastic new innovations in fertility treatment. But it didn't matter. We'd never have a kid that was half me, half her. We'd never go jogging together pushing our ridiculous three-wheeled buggy. We'd never have a troupe of singing blond kids, jumping up and down on our bed. It wasn't the end of the world, but it felt like the end of one type of life. The more she tried to comfort me the more I felt myself less of a man. In the end I couldn't bear her sympathy any longer.

I told her that I needed time alone. I thought I was being bold and selfless. A man's got to do what a man's got to do, I said as I loaded my bags in the car. She tried to get in touch, but I didn't return her calls. She confronted me at the office and, over the shouts of the ad team, I told her to please get on with her life. When I discovered she'd resigned, I congratulated myself. You've done the honorable thing, I thought.

To avoid going home, I started going out with the sales lads. I had plenty of time on my hands and they were always ready to join you for a few after-work drinks. To be able to handle these ever increasing binges, I'd follow them into the gents for a quick toot of the white stuff. It did the job for while. Getting home in the early hours, head fuzzy with pints and powder, helped me to ignore the voice that kept mocking me for being a useless jaffa whose genes had hit a brick wall. It was only when the editor called me into his goldfish bowl office and threatened to pull the chain on my career that it dawned on me. My life was now as empty as my flat. I'd been a total idiot.

Now, twelve months after I walked out, I stare at my notes and the headlines I've jotted down. 'How to balls up your relationship'. 'Shoot yourself dead with blanks'. 'Don't bank on your sperm'. I told my editor this feature would be easy to write. Fun yet informative. Perfect for our audience.

I was wrong. Writing about losing the only girl you've ever really loved is never easy, even if you do change the names. Natalie always said that if I carried on working for a stupid magazine, I'd turn stupid. Now I realise she was right. One by one, I rip the pages out of my pad, until all the words I've scrawled are crunched up in tight balls. I order another beer and begin to write something different. It's not a new feature. It's a letter. It's the letter I should have written her, a year ago today.

The Wrong Bus Girl

So there she is on the wrong bus, staring at me with a trace of a smile, and here I am at the bus stop, frozen. Two parallel worlds of thoughts and feelings, separated by a pane of scratched glass. I look at the wrong bus queue. It's a shuffling dozen long.

The old man last in the line nudges me and speaks loudly through a tobacco-tinted moustache. 'That girl's giving you the right eye, son.'

'She's really beautiful isn't she?'

'What a lovely smile,' he says.

There are five people left to get on the bus. If I follow them I will be hideously late and if I am late, I'll miss my job interview.

The old man nudges me. 'Is she your missus?'

Voices reach us from up front. The driver is arguing with a passenger.

'Afraid not,' I sigh.

'Say what, son?' He cups his hand to his ear.

I stare at her and speak very slowly, pronouncing each word with great care in the hope she can read my lips. 'She's not my missus, but I wish she were.'

The argument at the front has stopped. The shuffling has resumed. There are two people still to pay. The old man is one. He walks two steps forward. I follow then take one step back.

'Why so down in the mouth, son?'

'It's not fair, is it?'

'Speak up, lad.'

'This. Her and me. So close. Maybe meant for each other, maybe even brought together by fate and the bus going the wrong bloody way…'

Then it hits me. And it's so amazingly obvious that I start to laugh. I wrench open my bag and throw stuff out, handfuls of it.

The old man stares as he gets on the bus.

'Please, can you give her this?' I say, holding my business card out. 'To the girl. My missus who's not my missus, can you give it to her?'

'What?' he shouts. 'What did you say?'

I bellow my instructions at him and hand over the card. He takes it and shakes his head. 'Do I look like I'm in the market for life insurance, son?'

'No, I just work in insurance. I'm not selling it. Just give the card to the girl, the pretty girl. Understand?'

When he winks, I want to hug him.

The bus driver snarls at me. 'Getting on or not?'

I catch a glimpse of the girl, my girl, and smile. She smiles back. A big, proper smile, and I want to punch the sky. Then I see the right bus, the number 48, pulling up. The queue for it is only three long. I have no time to loiter.

The wrong bus driver revs his engine and asks me again if I'm getting on.

I grin and shake my head. 'No, thanks. You're going in the wrong direction.'

The bus pulls away and I wave goodbye to her. I actually wave. As if we're friends already. And she does the same. I point at the old man who has taken the seat in front of her and I mouth the words *say hello*. She shrugs and smiles as the bus moves into the traffic. And for a couple of seconds, I'm filled with such a feeling of joy that I sing out loud. Then, just before the bus turns the corner, I see the old man pull open the window and toss out a small white card. It flutters and spins and twirls, until it is sucked beneath a passing car. I stare at the bus turning away. I stare at the space where the bus was, where my card was, and where the girl was. I stare at the space for so long, that when the number 48 leaves, I'm not on it.

Opportunity Man

Marcus knew he still had the touch, no matter what Stella said. And Friday evening in Leicester Square, with the warm air on your skin and the crowd buzzing at the prospect of a good night out, was the perfect place to prove it. He'd lost count of how many girls he'd picked up for her on summer weekends like this. They came from all over. A Polish redhead looking to make a few quid, a jet-black Nigerian just off the plane, and a posh runaway who spoke like the Queen. He liked to tell them he was the Opportunity Man and, today, he was knocking on their door.

'You used to be a natural, a real artist. Now you've gone soft,' Stella said, when he reminded her of his successes.

'Don't be stupid! I'm still the business!'

But she carried on stuffing his Armani shirts into a Tesco bag and throwing his shoes in a box, anyway.

Truth was, things hadn't been going great. He had turned a couple of girls down because they reminded him of his little sister. Another because she said she had a kid. But there was no way he'd gone soft. Not in a million years.

Now, as he cruised through the crowds, he focused his attention on every single face. He was on his third circuit, when he spied a prospect. She was standing, arms folded, watching a busker playing guitar. Her spiky auburn hair, torn jeans and skanky T-shirt made her look like a punk kid. But with a bit of scrub, a haircut and some sexy clothes she had the potential to be a little goldmine.

He ambled closer and threw a quid in the busker's hat. The guy's eyes thanked him and he nodded back.

'He's got talent, hasn't he?'

The girl's gaze skitted over Marcus. 'He's okay.'

She had a slight accent. He couldn't place it, but she was no English girl, that was for sure.

He rubbed his hands together. 'You're not from around here, are you?'

'I'm Finnish.'

Shit. He didn't know jack about Finland. 'Cool! I hear it's a really beautiful country. Loads of snow, right?'

'Yes, snow all the time.' She examined her fingers. 'And we all live in igloos.'

Marcus laughed. Funny girl. He saw her nails were covered in specks of paint, just like the tatty army satchel she had over her shoulder. She had splashes of paint on her jeans too and a sketchpad sticking out of her bag. You didn't need to be Sherlock Holmes to see what she was into.

'Bet you're an artist, right?'

'How could you tell?'

At first he thought she was being sarcastic again, but her lips fought a smile and she looked at him with genuine interest. Beneath her make-up, he could now see she was younger than he'd first thought. Nineteen, twenty maybe. He grinned. It would make things easier.

'I can tell an artist a mile off,' he said, taking out a cigarette. 'My ex used to be a dancer.'

'Really, what sort?'

He clicked his heels and a clapped his hands. 'Flamenco.'

'Was she Spanish?'

'No, she was from Leeds. But she trained in Andalucia. When she moved her body to that Latino stuff, it made you forget everything.' He sighed. 'But you can't make any money doing that, so she had to do other stuff too. Bet it's the same for you, hey?'

'I am used to being without money.'

'Not nice though, is it?'

She shrugged.

'You know what, I might be able to help you out with a job.'

The girl tugged at her hair, doubtless remembering all the warnings she'd ever heard about strange men. But Marcus knew he didn't look strange. Stella reckoned that was why it was so easy for him to score.

'Trust me, honey,' she once said. 'With those soppy baby blues and girly eyelashes, they'll think it's Bambi offering them work.'

The girl sniffed. 'What sort of job?'

'Let me buy you a drink and I'll tell you all about it.' The offer hung in the air with the smell of cheap hotdogs and car fumes.

She checked her watch, then looked him up and down. 'Okay, but only if you let me sketch you.'

'What?'

'I want to draw your face.'

'Yeah?'

'You'd make a great subject.'

'You reckon?' He clicked his fingers for the first time since Stella had thrown him out.

'I do. You have a very fine bone structure.'

'Sold!' He held out his hand. 'Nice to meet you, Miss Artist. I'm Marcus.'

'Lotte,' she said.

Her grip was harder than he expected.

'Cigarette?'

She took two.

As he walked her to the bar, Marcus told her how much he loved the summer. He told her how it had been scientifically proven that the sun makes people happier, and how you could see it even by the way people walked. He told her that one day he'd move to Faro in Portugal, because that was Europe's sunniest place.

'In the north of Finland, it does not get dark at all for three months.'

'You're kidding me?' he said.

She shook her head. 'No, I'm not. People go crazy with all that light.'

'Maybe I should move there instead!'

When they reached the terrace, he pulled a chair out for her.

She sat down without thanking him and rummaged around in her bag.

'So what is this job you have for me?' she said, yanking out her pad.

He took off his jacket and rolled up his sleeves to show off his fake Rolex Steel.

'It's easy money for someone like you. My mate runs this gentlemen's club and he's looking for pretty girls to sell stuff to his clients. Drinks and cigarettes, things like that.'

'Sounds like a brothel.'

Sharper than she looks, he thought. 'No. No. It's nothing like that,' he said. 'Gentlemen's clubs are all the rage now. It's twenty-five quid an hour and you don't even need to wear bunny ears!'

A waitress interrupted them. Marcus could tell she recognised him by the way she blushed. He smiled, wondering how many girls she'd seen him with. Probably wouldn't believe him if he told her he'd been with one woman for nearly two years. Trying to shake himself free of Stella thoughts, he ordered a Whisky Mac and a Razzmatazz for Lotte.

'Twenty-five pounds an hour?' She pulled out a pencil and started flicking it across the pad. 'Plus tips?'

'Yeah, you'd clean up. Want to go and have a look? Get introduced to my mate?'

'Keep still!' she snapped. 'I can't draw if you move around so much.'

He did as he was told. 'You know you remind me of my girlfriend. She was a lot older, but otherwise…'

'Why are you talking about her in the past tense?' Lotte gazed at her pad. 'Did she meet someone else?'

'You could say that,' Marcus lied, remembering the day Stella told him that she'd found herself a replacement. The way she'd delivered the news, so matter of fact, she might as well have been talking about the weather. He was happy when the waitress returned. It was easier to focus on the present with a drink in hand.

'Cheers,' he said, lifting his glass.

'Cheers,' she said without looking up.

He stared at her while she worked. She was frowning, and the tip of her tongue poked out of her mouth. After a few minutes of silence, she picked up her cocktail and knocked it back. The movement was so sudden that he jumped.

'Did I scare you?' she said.

'Do all Finnish girls drink like that?'

'Only on Fridays.'

He studied her for a hint of a smile, but her lips were pressed in a thin line. Her gaze was totally focused on the pad. It was like trying to interpret the emotions of a rock.

'You keep staring. It's rude.' She held her pencil up, closed one eye and measured him. 'I do the staring, okay?'

He nearly mumbled an apology but took another swig of his drink instead. The way she looked at him was making him feel uncomfortable.

'You know what?' she said. 'I've never drawn a pimp before.'

'What are you talking about!'

'I might be foreign, but I am not stupid,' she said, continuing her sketch.

He slammed his drink down and looked around to see if anyone was listening. 'Look, I'm no pimp, okay. I'm the opportunity man.'

She laughed. 'Sounds like a bad superhero.'

He sucked his teeth. 'I'm not a superhero but I'm not a pimp either. I'm just helping my mate out.'

'Of course you are.'

He clenched his fists under the table. His foot tapped the pavement. 'Listen, sweetheart, I do this because I have to. It's my job, all right.'

'I think it is very sad. I think you are a fraud.'

'Why's that?'

'I can see what you are really like.' She hugged her pad and tapped it with her pencil. 'It's Finnish magic. Want to look?'

'Yeah, I do.'

'What is it worth?'

'What do you mean?'

'What's it worth to see you through my eyes?'

'I've just bought you a drink.'

'My vision of you is not so cheap. I want fifty pounds.'

'What?'

'Fifty pounds or you never know what I see.'

He paused. Was it possible this girl really did see him differently? She sure acted like she did. Stella would have bawled him to hell and back for doing something so stupid, but Stella was gone. He looked around to see if anyone was watching them, then pulled out his wallet and quickly passed her a fifty.

Lotte tossed the pencil on the table and spun the pad around.

He gazed at the sketch. It wasn't what he saw in the mirror every day. It was like looking at himself in soft focus. More boy than man.

'Why did you draw me like this?'

'This is how I see you.'

He stared at her. She didn't flinch. He lit another cigarette.

'Listen,' he said, 'I don't know what you're trying to pull, but I don't look like that. Got it?'

She ripped out the sketch and passed it to him. 'This is how you look to me. It is nothing to be ashamed of. Most English people I sketch are like you. Pretending to be something they are not. It is not healthy.' She packed her pad away and stood up. 'You should take the opportunity to be yourself, Mr Opportunity Man.'

'You have no idea what you're talking about!'

'I only draw what I see,' she said. 'Now, I have to go.'

He watched her walk into the crowd then sunk back into his chair and stared at the portrait. Tracing the lines of the pencil with his finger, he wondered how she'd done it. He carried on wondering until the waitress came to clear their glasses. She leaned over so close he could smell her almond perfume. He wanted to ask her what she thought of the drawing. Instead, scared of what she might say, he thanked her and strode back into the square.

It was as buzzing as ever. The crowds were still packed with prospects, the air still warm on the skin and Marcus still had a job to do. Yet somehow the square had changed. It didn't fill him with the same sense of opportunity it had just an hour before. He stood staring at people smiling. He listened to the laughter and the chatter. Then, when it became too much to bear, he lit a cigarette and walked away.

Buy Ma Biscuits Or Kiss Ma Fish

Out in the ocean, toward the horizon, a surfer rides a wall-sized wave. Nearer the shore, the sparkling heads of swimmers dive and surface; nearer still, at the ocean's edge, boys and girls unsure of the water wade in slowly, daring each other forward. And then, on a blue and white beach towel far from water, there's me, sweating as I hug my knees. The surfer skims across the wave, he flips his board one way then the other. Just when it seems he's tamed it and will ride it home, it catches him. His board spears the sky and I see his body falling into the fizzing white froth.

That's life, I think. That's *your* life, the voice in my head says. It's right. It's always right.

I return to my study of the girl sunbathing near me. I try to laze back, adjust my sunglasses and hope against hope that I look cool. She is only five yards away. Her hair is piled up in a soft black curl, her body, shining with oil, is covered by a stripy yellow-green bikini that is held together with nothing more than colourful bits of string.

Five yards away, and yet it feels so far. I'll not leave until I speak to her. Any minute now I'll ask her for a light. I don't normally smoke in the day, definitely not in this heat. But she's smoking, this beach goddess, and that's my way in. The cigarette I have been twirling through my fingers is all buckled and dirty, stained with sun-tan lotion, so I toss it aside and pull another from my packet.

Get real, says the voice in my head.

Thing is, this time I am real. It's all about timing. I'm a devout believer in this. If I time it right, she might say 'Yeah sure I've got a light' and then she might ask where I'm from and do I fancy meeting up later in this cute little beach bar she knows with star-shaped lamps and cocktails the size of flower pots.

Dream on, the voice says. Yeah, I do, I almost shout. I dream a

45

lot. I can fly with this as far as I like. We're on holiday in Mexico. Now we're in Copenhagen, drinking in a harbour bar. Now we're trashing the snowman we built to save it from the slow death of thawing. She's glowing with the cold, and she's laughing.

First, I need to speak to her. That's all I need to do. But there's a problem; I can't see her eyes. She is looking out across the ocean, wearing big wraparound shades that hide half her face. I need to see her eyes before I can make my move. For all I know, she is gawping at one of those pumped-up boys slicing across the sea on their boards. I snap my cigarette in half and grind it into the sand.

One of the surfers ambles past me. He is all pecks and tattoos, all bracelets and dreadlocks. If he wasn't carrying a surfboard, he'd just be a hippie with a tan. A hippie with a tan and a six-pack. He has no beer gut. None. I'm not a big drinker, but when I look down there are a couple of little baby rolls of fat. Staring at my belly, those little rolls shining with coconut suntan lotion, I get that dizzy feeling again.

I know it well. It's almost as frequent a companion as the voice. Apparently this feeling is the beginning of the downward spiral: that's how the doctor described it, as though the loathing that fills me is some sort of sadistic fairground ride. Think positive, he said, you're a young man with plenty to offer. I repeat this phrase, the way he told me to. I'm a young man with plenty to offer.

Yeah, the voice says. To liposuction professionals, maybe. I sigh and ease myself up from the sand. There's a whining in my head as I stand, and my legs feel good to buckle.

Loser, the voice says. Loser. I clench my fists and wait to see if it has any other words of wisdom for me, but for now it stays quiet. I know it's right. It always is. It told me I was shit at my job and should leave before they fired me, and it told me that Bella was too good for me and was playing around with my flatmate. It's so damn smug, knowing everything, but then it's easy for it to chirp away with these simple truths. It doesn't have to deal with the things I have to deal with.

Even with my eyes closed, the sunlight makes everything orange. I take a deep breath and hold it for a count of ten. Then slowly I exhale. It's a technique taught by my old sales trainer, meant to prepare us for big presentations. Of course that's not something I need to worry about anymore, but it does the job and I feel my body relax. Opening my eyes I see that the girl has turned round and seems to be looking directly at me.

I want to run away. I want to bury myself in the sand. Instead, I look over her head as if I haven't even seen her, stick out my arms and attempt to do a Tai Chi thing with my hands. Weaving them between each other, I imagine that I'm dancing at a club and slowly playing with the strobes.

What the hell do you look like? says the voice. She's going to think you're a right twat.

I don't know if it's the power of the sun or the sound of the sea, or both, but I manage to ignore it. When, eventually, she looks the other way, I drop to my knees, sweating more than I have all day.

I know life wasn't always like this, but when I try to remember how it was before, it's like trying to recall a film I watched when I'd had too much to drink. It's pointless dwelling on the past, that's another of the doctor's classics, but sometimes the present is just so tiring. I have an urge to curl up in a ball and nuzzle the sand, or to walk steadily into the sea.

The voice usually keeps quiet if I stay still and do nothing. I could maybe just sit here and carry on watching the girl. The thought makes me blush. Perhaps I should just go to bed, neck a couple of pills and wait for tomorrow.

'Buy ma biscuits or kiss ma fish! Buy ma biscuits or kiss ma fish!'

For a second, I think it's the voice, messing around with me. So, when I spot a woman waddling across the beach, a box stuffed with cookies balanced on her head and a dead puffer fish in her hand, I grin. She wears a yellow smock so bright it looks like her dark head is fixed to a body made of gold. I must be staring, because she flashes me a big grin. I smile back.

47

'Wanna kiss my fish?' she says.

I shake my head, gazing at the dead thing she swings in front of my face. It looks like a grey football with fat lips and spikes. 'I'm not that desperate,' I say.

She laughs. Her chin wobbles. 'Then you gotta buy my biscuits. That's the deal. Biscuit or fish, your choice.'

The smell of that rotting fish is making me gag. 'What if I don't want either?'

'Listen, junior. Sometimes life gives you difficult choices. So you can kiss this or eat one of these. That's not difficult, is it?' She shows me a biscuit with chocolate chunks as big as pennies.

'What other flavours have you got?'

'I got choccy, I got coconut, I got cinnamon. I got everything.'

Over her shoulder I can see the girl. She has taken her glasses off and is looking at us. She has eyes as green as glass, almost too big for her face.

I lean closer to the woman. 'What do you think that girl over there would like?'

The woman glances round. 'She's a coconut girly. For sure.'

'You reckon?'

'I know a coconut girly when I see one, and she one all over.'

She doesn't know shit, the voice says.

'Okay,' I say. 'Give me one coconut.'

My hand shakes as I pass her the money. She grabs my palm in hers. I'm surprised how soft it is. 'You don't need to get yourself in a tizzy. I tell you she's a coconut girly then she is,' she says, giving my hand a squeeze.

She doesn't know what she is talking about, the voice shouts. The voice makes me jump. It's loud, angry.

The woman stares into my eyes. 'Listen, junior, if she ain't a coconut girly, I'll kiss ma own fish. Right here, in front of the whole damn beach.'

The girl is still watching us. I take a deep breath and take a step towards her. I hold the coconut biscuit flat upon my palm, and now the ache comes, twisting my stomach. I bite my lip and take two more steps. The girl is staring at me, not smiling, not anything.

You look like a loser, the voice says. I shake my head, trying to shut it up; another step, and then I freeze. It's as far as I can go. It's good enough, I think. I tried. I did something. The girl starts to turn away. Yes, the voice says, you did well. Now sit down and be quiet.

'Remember, I'll kiss it, I'm gonna kiss it for you!' the woman shouts.

Hearing her, I stumble forward and I'm there by the girl's side. She looks up at me. I swallow hard. I wish I'd never bothered, wish I'd just gone back to my room, blacked out the windows and sunk into bed. Now it's too late. I will humiliate myself again. I want to throw the biscuits at the woman, but instead I hold out the cookie. Crumbs drop through my fingers.

'Do you like coconut?' I say.

'What?' the girl says

'Do you – I thought you liked coconut?'

She looks at the biscuit and then looks me up and down and I'm waiting for the sand to cave in and the sea to wash me away. I want to punch myself for being so stupid and the doctor for telling me to take a little break and the woman for saying she will kiss her fish. Then her hand reaches towards mine, and with delicate fingers she plucks the cookie from my palm. She smiles.

'Yeah, as it happens. How did you know?' she says.

I shrug. 'I just knew.'

'I'll share it with you if you want?'

I nod and drop to my knees, though my mouth is too dry to eat. The woman shuffles past, swinging her fish. She waves it at me and I grin back. My mouth hurts with the strength of it. Even when a surf boy struts past, the smile doesn't go away. I wait for the voice to tell me that I look like a prick, that the girl will think I'm a moron if I don't stop grinning like a clown and say something to her. But she's eating the cookie, and I'm still smiling, and the voice doesn't say a single word.

The Cost of Advertising

I rummage through my wardrobe and pick out my sharpest suit. It's single breasted, charcoal coloured with a slight retro feel. Next, I take a black shirt, chunky silver cufflinks and a black tie from Kenzo that cost seventy quid. Fashion is an essential component for every advertising salesman. A cool looks says, I'm a player, someone you want on your side. Of course, it's not certain to swing a deal your way, nothing is, but it can sure tip the balance. And today, I need all the help I can get.

Once dressed, I study myself in the mirror. Too many long lunches and late nights have taken their toll. My eyes are puffy and my skin is blotchy. I rub moisturiser on the affected areas. My head is shaved a number three, which mean no messing around with gel or wax or blow-drying. This gives me approximately ten extra minutes to manage my goatee. Some days I imagine what it would look like if I let the hair go wild and burst forth from my face like a modern day mountain man. When I've had a good month and a fat commission cheque, I picture myself with something akin to a Salvador Dalí moustache. But it's all a dream. When you're in my business, you don't have the same leeway with facial hair as wandering woodsmen and eccentric artists.

Salla says I take my appearance too seriously. She says it's only a job, but then she's from Finland, where the only people who wear suits are bankers and insurance men. Plus, she's got no idea I'm saving money to marry her in style. What she does know is how to knock up a fantastic breakfast. Unfortunately, last night she stayed at her place, so rather than eggs on toast and fresh orange, I start the day with a Marlboro Light and a biscuit Boost.

Outside, it feels as if the sun can't be bothered. People march with their heads down. Cars belch and growl. Even though I sell advertising for *Cool Car Lovers*, the country's second most popular car mag, I hate the way traffic clogs up the streets and fouls the air. I wonder if the single drivers, alone in their five-seater cars, feel any guilt because every single one of them is frowning.

Things are no different at the Underground station. When the tube arrives it's so full of people it looks like an attempt at a Guinness world record. By the time I get to Oxford Street, one side of my suit is already crumpled. I'd smooth it down, but with only three minutes left before the clock strikes nine, I have to sprint through Soho. I arrive at my desk with my tie askew and sweat puddling behind my ears.

Darren looks at his watch.

'Afternoon,' he says. 'Early morning workout at the gym?'

'Very funny.' I sit down, quickly unpack my bag and turn my computer on. 'Is Miranda in yet?'

'Haven't heard her.' Darren leans forward. 'She was out on a bender last night, though. I saw her in Blue Lounge, then in the Doghouse. I left at one and she was still on the fizzy.'

'Oh shit! She's coming with me to see Tom Harcourt at Zoom today.'

Darren sucks his teeth. 'What, the guy who's banging the Sales Manager of *Your Car*?'

I nod. 'Miranda wants to know why he's put all BMW's money in his girlfriend's mag instead of ours.'

'Well, you don't have to be a rocket scientist to work that out.'

Before I can answer, I see Miranda striding towards me. She looks like she's just stepped off a catwalk. Her hair is all done up in ringlets, she's wearing a frilly white blouse, pantaloons and knee-high boots with dangerously pointed toes. If she had a rapier, you might mistake her for a female musketeer. Darren starts tapping on his computer.

I sit up straight and stick my chest out.

'On flexitime, Eliot?' she asks.

'What do you mean?'

'You're late yet again.'

54

'Maybe a fraction, depending upon which clock you look at.'

She glares at me with her mascara-ringed eyes. 'This isn't a game. You need to pick up the pace, otherwise you'll have nothing to be late for.'

I'm tired of her threatening me, but nod nonetheless.

'I expect you to be ready to go in half an hour,' she says.

'But the meeting's not until ten.'

'One,' she says, holding up a finger tipped with a rose-red nail, 'I am never late. Two, arriving early is a sign of professionalism. I'd hoped you'd have learnt that by now.'

I nod again. Seemingly satisfied with my response, she walks off.

'Fuck me, you must have really pissed her off,' Darren says. 'What did you do?'

I'd like to share my theory with him, but what's the point? Instead I shrug, and go for a wander to get my head clear. The office doesn't help. It's open plan and decorated with primary colours. Harsh neon light reflects off the glass walls of the meeting rooms. I've always assumed this combination is a result of some theory in interior design. Maybe it's meant to increase productivity. If so, it doesn't work for me. It feels as if I spend my day on the set of a Saturday morning children's television show.

I start to get my stuff together for the meeting. When my bag is packed with circulation certificates, media packs, old issues of *Cool Car Lovers*, my phone, my laptop and my business cards, I make my way to reception. Miranda's already there.

'Where's our taxi?' she asks.

'I thought we could walk.'

'How very environmentally sound of you.'

I don't bother replying. Instead, I go out into the street and hail a cab.

As we drive, sitting in silence, I wonder what would've happened if I'd have said yes to her at Darren's birthday party. We'd taken over the downstairs of the Slug and Lettuce. It had been a fun night, with fizzy freely flowing thanks to commission cheque generosity and Miranda's card behind the bar. I was quietly smoking a cigarette outside when she swanned up to me, and held out her hand.

'Just what I need.'

I pulled open the packet and handed her one.

'Light?'

I flicked open my Zippo. She wrapped her hands around mine and I noticed her pupils were the size of chocolate buttons.

'Do you have a girlfriend, Eliot?' she asked.

'Yeah.'

'Living together?'

'Not yet.'

'How old is she?'

'A couple of years younger.'

'Ever tried a real woman?'

'What do you mean?'

'Follow me around the corner and you'll find out.'

I stood there staring at the space she'd inhabited, wondering whether she really meant it, or whether it was just coke talk. It didn't matter. Miranda might be beautiful and she might be my boss, but even with half a bottle of champagne fizzing away at my rationality, I knew I could never do it. Not to Salla. Not to the only girl I'd ever truly loved. I didn't go back to the party. Instead, I wandered through the streets hoping the episode would be forgotten in the morning. The next day Miranda called me into her office and, with a smile I thought meant I'd been forgiven, gave me the BMW account.

The memory makes me twitchy. The leather seat squeaks. Miranda tuts and carries on staring out the window. It's a relief when the cabbie spins the wheel round in his meaty hands and we pull up in front of a tall Georgian town house with the words Zoom stretched across its entrance. Miranda leaves me to pay.

The person who did our office seems to have got his hands on Zoom's reception, too. It feels as if I'm sitting in a rainbow. The walls are littered with adverts and framed certificates heralding the creative genius of the agency. Table football stands next to the sofa. The coffee counter is a cloud shaped fish tank with a glass cover.

These are exactly the type of furnishings that advertising agencies always dazzle their clients with. The sad thing is that it works. The first time I ever went into an agency reception, I was blown away. I couldn't believe how cool it was. It felt more like the chill out room of a club than an office. I remember thinking how lucky I was to work in such an exciting industry. This feeling lasted almost a year, until I met Salla. It was her who first suggested that advertising might not be as glamorous as I thought.

'It's all a bit of a waste, don't you think?' she said one night.

'What do you mean?'

She rolled one lock of sunshine-coloured hair around her finger. 'A waste of talent. All these artists and writers using their skills to persuade people to buy junk they don't need.'

I laughed. 'Another classic commie insight from Red Salla.'

She lobbed a cushion at me. 'There's nothing socialist about that. It's just common sense.'

Despite my teasing, she got me thinking. She was good at that.

If she were with me now and could see Tom Harcourt emerging from behind a pink fluffy door wearing combat trousers and a T-shirt with the word 'Talent' splashed across the chest, she'd doubtless feel vindicated. I, on the other hand, just feel overdressed. Miranda stands up to present her cheek, which Tom dutifully air kisses. I reach out my hand.

'How's it going, fella?' he says.

'Brilliantly,' I say.

'Great. I've booked Jackson Pollock for us.'

'Sorry?'

'The Jackson Pollock room.' He laughs, sounding like an excited pig. 'Our meeting rooms are all named after the twentieth century's greatest creatives. There's the John Lennon, the Andy Warhol, the Virginia Woolf…'

'Very clever,' Miranda says.

'Inspired,' I say.

'Inspiration is our business, fella.'

The Jackson Pollock room is, as you would expect, splattered. Even as I sit down, I feel a headache coming on. I can't imagine a place more likely to cause migraines. Miranda takes a chair at the head of the table, I place myself between her and Tom. His cologne smells of marzipan. I notice he hasn't shaved.

'So, what's happening with BMW,' I say and pull out my laptop.

'Oh please, not another PowerPoint,' he says. 'If I have to sit through another slideshow this week, my head will explode.'

'It'd help me show you how our readership compares with BMW's target group.'

'I know everything there's to know about your magazine's readers.'

'Well, then you'll know it has a greater percentage of AB1 males than any other car magazine.' I glance at Miranda, expecting her to lend some support. She says nothing.

'Listen, fella, who was it that said statistics are nothing more than lies and damned lies?'

'Pretty sure Mark Twain said something like that.'

Tom beamed. 'So great minds do indeed think alike.'

'We spend hundreds of thousands of pounds on our circulation.'

'I'm sure you do, but I rely on gut feeling. It says *Your Car* provides the best vehicle for my client to reach their core audience.'

I want to shout that it also provides you with the best vehicle to get a fuck, on a regular basis, but I restrain myself. From the corner of my eye, I can see Miranda shaking her head. I decide to play my joker.

'Perhaps we could discuss BMW's contingency budget over lunch.'

'Where do you have in mind?'

'How does Jezzo's sound?'

'Right on, fella. There might be a tad left in the pot for special deals. I'll just pop upstairs and grab my jacket.'

I'm amazed at the speed at which he leaves the room.

'Brilliant. A textbook example of how to overcome an objection,' Miranda says.

'I had no choice.'

'What do you mean you had no choice? Perhaps you could've tried selling some of the benefits of our magazine.'

'You know his girlfriend works on *Your Car*.'

'Don't give me excuses, Eliot. You've already had a warning about your attitude. You have to get BMW back into *Cool Car Lovers*, simple as that.'

'He says there might be something left in the pot.'

'Let's hope so for your sake.'

Tom bounces back into the room. He's wearing a Parka jacket with a massive furry hood. It makes him look like a cross between a Britpop guitarist and an arctic explorer.

'Have you called to book a table, fella?'

'Good point,' I say.

I pull out my iPhone with Union Jack cover, making sure Tom gets an eyeful, and flick through my address book.

'You don't happen to have their number, do you?' I ask him.

'Hang on, I'll just check.' He pulls out of a slick blue smartphone that looks like it's been beamed from the future.

He sees me staring at it. 'Pretty damn neat, hey? Nokia's latest Lumia. Don't know how I survived without it.'

'Are they all blue?'

'It's cyan, fella. They come in a bundle of colours, but this goes with my eyes, don't you think?' He flutters his lashes and laughs.

Miranda laughs, too. I grin even though it hurts.

He holds the phone to his mouth and says Jezzo. It emits a call tone and I cringe as Tom asks for a table in the pricey downstairs restaurant rather in the cheaper upstairs brasserie.

'Job done,' he says.

We squeeze into another cab. Miranda and Tom take the big seat and I'm left to perch on the little flip-down stool. Miranda throws the names of exotic holiday locations around like confetti. Tom is congratulating her on being such an adventurer while dropping in his own experiences of far-away places. I'd bet my next commission cheque that even if these two went away to a jungle in Borneo or a desert in Uzbekistan, they'd find a five star Sheraton to stay in.

'Where are you jetting off to next, fella?'

'Blackpool,' I say. 'I can't get enough of the lights.'

'Oh, right. Cool. You're doing the northern thing?'

'Yeah, I go every year. I don't know what it is about the place that just keeps drawing me back. It just has this magical quality.'

Miranda is puckering her face at me, so I shut up. She knows that last year I went to Croatia and not Blackpool, because she was the one who gave me the time off. Tom is scratching his head. He seems lost for words. This makes me feel happier than I've felt all morning. When we arrive, I'm left to pay the cabbie again.

Jezzo's is all glass, big lights, gold furnishings and noise. Miranda and Tom have already been taken to the table, so I wander over.

'Can I help you, Sir?' a waiter says in a voice that makes him sound as though he's gay, but trying to be French.

'I'm with them,' I say.

He raises two perfectly plucked eyebrows. 'Oh, I see. I thought Sir and Madam were a couple. Please take a seat, I will be with you in a moment.'

Miranda and Tom don't even bother to acknowledge my arrival. As this is my final chance to win Tom over, I decide to throw caution to the wind and go for the most expensive dishes on offer. The trouble is, like most of the restaurants in Soho, Jezzo's endorses the law of diminishing returns. The more you pay, the less food you get. Taken to its logical extremes, if I were to pay a thousand quid for a starter, I'd be served a crumb on a plate the size of a satellite dish. I wait until they've ordered their food and then bring up BMW again.

'So, you were saying that BMW might have a bit tucked away for special deals.'

'To be honest with you, fella, it'd have to be real special.'

'We've got a luxury car supplement coming up next month, and between you and me, I suspect BMW will be getting some very good editorial coverage.'

'I should hope so. They're one of the world's leading car brands.'

'Which is exactly why they should be in one of the world's leading car magazines.'

'They are. *Your Car.*'

I look at Miranda. She is leaning back in her chair, arms crossed.

'You and I both know that in terms of reputation, circulation and editorial coverage, *Your Car* can't compare to *Cool Car Lovers*,' I say.

He shrugs. 'All good things come to an end.'

'Listen, if I put together an attractive package for the next issue, would you be interested?'

'Can't guarantee it, fella, but I'll take a look.'

The discussion comes to an end when the waiter asks me if I want to taste the wine. I say yes, but what I'd really like to do is pour it over Tom's head. By just having a look, Tom might just as well have doffed a black cap and condemned my career and future happiness with Salla to the gallows.

I take a swig of the thick red liquid. It's nice and fruity with a slight peppery taste. I know nothing about wines, so I'm not sure if this is how it's meant to taste, but I tell the waiter it's fine. He gives me a look that says, I know you're a fraud. He must be used to that. At lunchtime, this place is full of suits on corporate lunches, living it up on other people's cash. I watch as he fills Miranda's glass. She makes no effort to stop him.

'Thanks, fella,' Tom says once his glass is full.

'Joel,' the waiter says.

'Sorry, fella?'

'My name's Joel.'

'Oh, right, nice one. I always thought that was a French girl's name.'

'It's unisex.'

'Lucky you,' Tom says and winks.

The waiter looks confused and asks whether we're ready to order. I stick with my original choice. Tom goes for the same while Miranda, telling us she's got to look after her figure, has a rocket salad followed by baby chicken. Tom says her figure must be a pleasure to look after, which earns him a big smile. I make a toast to put an end to the sickening compliments. Tom downs half his glass in one and excuses himself to go to the gents.

'So far, so bad,' Miranda says.

'He says he's willing to have a look at a proposal.'

'We both know what that means.'

'You have to give me a chance to put something on paper for him.'

'You've had plenty of chances. If you'd have taken them when they were offered, things might be different.'

'It was nothing personal, Miranda. I have a girlfriend. I love her and I want to marry her,' I say trying to appeal to her heart.

She laughs. 'I was after a quick snog, not a diamond ring.'

Tom struts back to the table, sniffling. Miranda stares in his direction. He smiles back.

'That's better,' he says, clapping his hands together. 'Food arrived yet? Once, when I was lunching at the Oxo Tower, it took nearly an hour for my starter to arrive. I'm a patient kinda guy, but that's just taking the piss. Do you know what I mean, fella?'

Before giving me the chance to answer, he turns to Miranda. 'I bet they wouldn't dare do that to a beautiful lady like you, not in a million years. I'm normally really into the Oxo Tower, it's got incredible views, and the…'

I switch off. His visit to the toilet appears to have given him a sudden burst of energy. I strongly suspect this is down to chemical stimulation. Miranda obviously has similar beliefs, as she is now held rapt by Tom's babbling, probably hoping he will sort her out later. Not that she needs sorting out if she can wait a few hours. Handily, we have our very own in-house dealer, 'Charlie' Peters. He's meant to work on admin, but most of his Excel spreadsheets concentrate on who owes him what. He's the most popular man in the building.

Ever since I've been saving for Salla's ring, I've reined in my urges, which is probably good for me and for her. She says there's nothing more tedious on the planet than an Englishman with a head full of Colombian marching powder. Listening to Tom, I totally understand where she's coming from.

The starters arrive, and true to form, mine is so small it takes me only two mouthfuls to empty my large white plate. Tom hasn't stopped talking long enough to eat his. Miranda pushes her food around, seemingly gripped by Tom's latest topic of conversation, the injustices of the football play-off system.

The thought of him getting wasted while wrecking my life makes my heart beat faster and my neck sweat. I undo my tie and down the rest of my wine. When Tom announces that he doesn't know what's wrong with his bladder but needs to go to the gents again, I give him a few seconds head start, take a deep breath and get up to follow him.

'Where you going?' Miranda says.

'I need the loo, too.'

'I hope that's all you need.'

I ignore her and make my way to the toilet. The marble, black wood theme makes me feel like I've just walked back into the 80s. Only one cubicle is closed. I enter the one next door, stand on the toilet seat and poke my head over the partition. Tom is busy chopping up two fat white lines with his gold card. I duck back down and pull out my mobile. My hand shakes a little as I turn on the camera. I sneak my head back over and film Tom rolling up a twenty quid note and snorting the lines. When he's finished, he flicks his head as if in a shampoo advert, only to freeze half way when his eyes catch mine.

'What the fuck are you doing, fella?' he says, dusting the toilet seat in panic.

'Just admiring your technique.'

He gives a nervous laugh. 'What's with the phone?'

I jump off the toilet seat. My heart's pumping faster than ever, but I feel good. I bounce on my toes. 'Sorry, I've got no choice. I filmed you. I need money to marry my girlfriend and you're getting in my way.'

Tom steams out of the cubicle and squares up to me.

'I hope you're not threatening me, fella.'

'I'm just telling you how it is. I need you to book an ad campaign in my magazine.'

'And what if I don't.'

I wave my phone. 'You know how easily videos go viral these days,' I say and walk out.

When I sit down, Miranda scrutinises my eyes. Tom returns to the table frowning. He glares at me and bangs his knife on the plate.

'Where the fuck is that lady boy?' he says.

'Who are you talking about?' Miranda asks.

'The idiot French queer we have as a waiter.'

'He's not an idiot. He's a nice guy just trying to do his job. And what do you need him for anyway? You've not even finished your starter yet,' I say.

Tom gulps the rest of his Châteauneuf du Pape. 'Maybe not, but I've finished my drink.'

Unsurprisingly, the meal goes downhill after that. Tom gets increasingly agitated and Miranda, arriving at the conclusion that Tom won't be offering her a pick me up, gets increasingly bored. We don't bother with dessert, much to the relief of our waiter, who's become the brunt of Tom's anger. When I pay, I apologise and give him a large tip.

Miranda demands another cab despite the office being a mere five minutes walk. While she waits inside, I shake hands with Tom. He squeezes my palm hard.

'I want a booking for twenty-four BMW pages in *Cool Car Lovers* by the end of the day,' I say.

'Nobody blackmails Tom Harcourt,' he says, pumping my hand harder.

'I'm sorry, really I am. But I have no other choice.'

I watch him stride up the street. It's a relief when he disappears from sight. The adrenaline rush I felt earlier has disappeared. Now I just feel a little drunk and a bit stupid. Miranda, on the other hand, looks like she spent lunchtime watching paint dry. She doesn't say anything until the cab drops us off at the office.

'Well, that was an utter waste of time.'

'Oh, I don't know about that.'

'You screwed it up, Eliot. Something of a forte of yours, isn't it.'

I shrug, suddenly feeling too tired to argue.

'You know I've been told to reduce my headcount, don't you,' she sighs. 'Not something I enjoy. In fact, I hate it. But if it's not you then it's going to be someone else.'

'What! You're sacking me?'

'No. I'm recommending you for redundancy. Chris makes the final decision.' She squeezes my arm. 'It's nothing personal. You just screwed up with one of our biggest accounts, that's all.'

When I get back to my desk, I bash out an email to Tom telling him he's got an hour to make his decision. I wonder how long it will take for him to respond. He could still call my bluff, in which case I'd be screwed. Despite my bravado at lunch, I could never follow through with my threat. Salla says that the salesman thing is like a suit of armour, which I use to hide my real feelings from the outside world.

'In Finland men try to protect themselves from getting hurt by saying too little. In England men do it by saying too much,' she says. 'Both ways are stupid.'

She's probably right. She often is. Whatever the answer, destroying a stranger's life really isn't my style. I go for a walk around the office to calm my nerves. It's then I see through the glass wall that Miranda is in our MD's office. They're deep in conversation. Chris looks taut, as if he could spring at me any minute. I scuttle away, thinking how I'm going to tell Salla I'm unemployed.

It's getting to the time in the afternoon when people are readying themselves to leave for home. There's not the same buzz fizzling through the air as when everyone's charged on caffeine and optimism. We're always told that mornings are prime selling time, which suggests to me that afternoons are not. When I sit down, Darren's at his desk.

'Tom Harcourt rang,' he says.

'Why didn't you get me?'

'I didn't know where you were.'

'What did he say?'

'He said to tell you to go fuck yourself.'

'Yeah, very good, funny man. What did he really say?'

'Look, I even wrote it down.' He holds up a post it note. 'He said he's sending you an email. Meeting clearly didn't go great then.'

'I've had better.' I slump in my chair. I have a strange hollow sensation in my stomach. I stare at my desk. It's a mess. I've never been the most organised person, but now I find myself eager for some order in my space. I grab a pile of papers and stuff them into my drawer. The sight of the wooden surface makes me feel a bit better, so I clear away some more. Darren asks me if I'm all right.

Before I can answer, my phone rings. It's Miranda.

'Can I see you in Chris's office? We'd like a word.'

Just as I get up, I see that Tom's email's arrived. I go to click it open, when Miranda sticks her head out of the door and bawls at me to hurry. The whole office stops what they're doing. Every head turns in my direction. I feel as if I'm walking the plank in front of a football crowd. It's a relief when she closes the glass door.

'Afternoon Eliot, take a seat,' Chris says without looking up.

I slide into the chair.

'I hear you went to see Zoom today,' he says, finally lifting his head.

'Yeah,' I say, unable to form a more complex sentence.

'I hear it didn't go very well.'

'I wouldn't necessarily say that. Tom has agreed to look at a proposal for the luxury car supplement.'

'And that's good enough, is it? BMW is a world-renowned brand. Do you know what it does to the reputation of *Cool Car Lovers* when we fail to carry a single page of their advertising?'

'It doesn't look very good,' I say.

'Too damn right it doesn't!'

'Your Sales Director tells me we used to have market share on BMW, before you took it over.'

'That's not fair. I've only had it for…'

'Life's not fair. She also tells me you have an attitude problem. We haven't got room for slackers in this company. Are you a slacker, Eliot?'

'No, I'm not. I work as hard as anyone here, including my Sales Director.'

I expect this final act of courage to be the end.

'Prove it,' Miranda says. 'Get your sales sheet for the month.'

I'm so surprised by this reprieve that I thank her. Word must have got out already because when I walk back through the office, sixty pairs of eyes follow me. I ignore them and begin rummaging round my desk. Then I remember Tom's email.

'You are a fucking arsehole,' it says. 'However, having gone through the circulation figures and analysed the editorial, I've come to the conclusion that *Cool Car Lovers* represents a better proposition for my client. Consequently, I've decided to book twenty-four exclusive pages in your magazine. I expect premium positions.'

I lick my lips as I click open the attachment. It's an order form worth one hundred and thirty eight thousand pounds. I bang the keys of my calculator. The little numbers tell me I've just earned over four and a half thousand pounds in commission. Enough to buy Salla the biggest ring I can find. I lean back in my chair and raise my arms aloft in silent celebration.

'What's the matter with you?' Darren says. 'Too much vino at lunchtime?'

'No. Well, maybe a little,' I savour the moment for a few more seconds, and print off the order form before returning to Chris's office.

'Let's have a look, then,' he says.

'Sorry, I couldn't find my folder.'

'This is exactly what I mean by attitude,' Miranda says. 'You ask him to do one simple thing and he screws it up.'

'Would you call twenty-four exclusive pages a screw up?'

'What?' she says. 'You wouldn't know twenty-four pages if they came up and slapped you in the face.'

'Miranda, please. This is not a playground,' Chris says and takes the sheet of paper off me. His expression doesn't change as he reads it. 'Well, I must say, I'm impressed. It seems your meeting wasn't quite the disaster I was led to believe. We've never got exclusive business from BMW before. This obviously makes the rest of our conversation pointless. If you wouldn't mind, I now need to have a word with your Sales Director alone. I'll be announcing your success to the rest of the company tomorrow morning. Excellent work, Eliot. Keep it up.'

I thank Chris and strut out, flashing Miranda a smile as I go. She looks away and starts fidgeting with her pen. Darren's nowhere in sight when I get back to my desk, so I put my hands behind my head and wallow in the warm glow of success. They say fortune favours the brave, and I congratulate myself on proving this proverb correct. I think about my talents being broadcast to the entire sales team tomorrow, a sales team that's probably expecting to hear about my imminent departure. I can't stop smiling.

I try to remember the last time I was bigged up in public. It was more than half a lifetime ago, when I was eleven and had come third in the county cross-country championship. It dawns on me that there's no way tomorrow will be the same. Not because I haven't done something worthy of praise. In our world, twenty-four exclusive BMW pages is the equivalent of an Olympic gold in cross-country. It's the manner of my victory. When I came third in that race, I ran so hard I thought I'd die, but getting these pages was nothing to do with skill or hard work.

I ponder that thought for what seems like a very long time. I try to imagine what Salla would say if I tell her what I've done today. I see her eyes looking at the floor, at her hands, anywhere but at me. She will kiss me, maybe, but I doubt she'll say a word. Sometimes, she's told me before, she thinks it's better to keep quiet.

I pull my keyboard closer and, with one finger, start to type. I feel like I'm writing a love letter to a girl I've lusted after for ages, yet never had the courage to tell. However, the email address is Miranda's and the title is 'Letter of resignation'. I hesitate for a second longer, enjoying the prickle of excitement, then click send.

For some reason I expect something to happen immediately. A fanfare or an eruption of fireworks, but all I see are people getting their stuff together and drifting out of the office. I look at my watch, it's five thirty-four. The working day's been over for four minutes and I'm still here. I switch my computer off and grab my bag. If I run, I might still get the six twelve from Vauxhall, but I'm tired of running. Instead, I amble through the office and out onto the street, all the time wondering whether the ring I buy her or the news I've packed my job in will make Salla smile more. Whatever the answer, one thing is for sure. Tomorrow I'll be spending ten extra minutes in bed with her rather than trimming my goatee.

Five Reasons For Leaving

Oliver pressed his forehead against the window pane. Snow was falling so hard that all he could see was the soft orange fizz of the road lamps and the white-grey shadows of people on the street below. Three sixteen and already dark. He wondered if there was any place more depressing to have found a note entitled 'Five reasons for leaving' and came up as blank as the sky.

It wasn't just that the darkness hoarded the days in winter, it was how it sucked your energy away, sponging off you like some dodgy friend you know will never pay you back. That was one reason he'd kept the TV on since Sanna left. It was a constant source of light and sound, even if he had no idea what the sound meant.

He drew a heart in the condensation and watched it dribble away as the flakes got fatter and fell faster. Snow used to be something to get excited about. It used to mean a day off work, or power cuts or snowball fighting till your arms ached. Now it meant he was miles away from home, and he had a decision to make.

Perhaps he should turn the TV off and put on some of his favourite tunes. They always helped him think better, but his CDs were already packed. He kicked his rucksack. It was nearly full, yet it still wasn't much for over a year up here on top of the world. He kicked the bag again, harder. It represented defeat. It represented going back to London life loveless, with an engagement ring he'd never show and a song he'd never sing. It meant being proved wrong and his mum and dad and his mates being proved right. You can't live up there. You'll hate it. You'll freeze to death. You'll never learn the lingo. You'll never get a job. You'll regret leaving the band forever.

He walked over to the table, where the note lay like a glove slapped around his face and then left as a challenge. Five reasons, he presumed, in no particular order. If he could truthfully refute them he'd go and ask her to marry him. That's what he'd decided when he'd first discovered the empty apartment, one day, eight hours and forty-three minutes earlier.

He sat down and stared at the lights Sanna had strung up for Christmas. They were not very festive. Yellow bathtub ducks with lipstick-red grins never made him feel merry. No doubt if his friends had visited him (which they hadn't, not once, despite their promises) they would have asked him if it was some bizarre Nordic tradition, like the ice-hole fishing or mushroom hunting or sweating to death in the sauna.

No, he would have told them, Sanna just loves ducks. She collects them. There are fluffy ones in the bed, ones that stick to the fridge, teapot ducks with a spout for a beak. Oliver didn't mind ducks. He'd even bought her one when they first met. Pulled it out in the World's End in Camden, over a pint of Stella. Pink and yellow china with big painted eyelashes.

'Here you go. I saw this on the market, and I thought, that has Sanna written all over it.' He held it aloft, presenting it for her inspection. 'What do you think?'

'You, Oliver Crane,' she said, wiping froth from her top lip, 'have an eye for ducks.'

'That's not all he's got an eye for, sweetheart,' the barman said, winking.

'No,' Oliver said, deadpan. 'I have an eye for swans, too.'

She laughed for the first time, and he knew even then he wanted to hear that sound over and over again.

Yeah, ducks were his way to her heart. One way. Yet despite indulging her, he apparently didn't like them with a sufficient passion. How did he know this? It was the first of her five reasons for leaving him. Not the most kicking-in-the-gut reason, not by a long shot. But it was still the first. 'You hate my ducks' there in black and white as if she were three rather than thirty-three.

Maybe she was just warming up or maybe it was something symbolic, he thought, tracing the letter with his finger. Sanna had a Masters in Psychology and loved to fill his head with her mumbo jumbo. Freud this, Jung that. Hating her ducks was probably something to do with his messed-up childhood.

He banged the table. If they'd still been in London, he'd have at least had his piano, now sold to pay for the first month's rent. He could have pounded away at the keys.

'I miss the way you frown when you read,' he said. His voice sounded like an old friend who'd started smoking. 'I miss stroking the soft skin on the inside of your arm. I miss kissing the little pointed peaks of your ears. I miss the smell of your hair.'

He stopped. His words sounded like the lyrics to a bad song, but it was true. He really did miss those things. He held the note in his hand. The writing was beautiful. He'd always been jealous of Sanna's ability to make the most mundane look like art. Collages of newspaper clippings, birthday cards fashioned from book covers and tinsel, painted T-shirts.

The second reason, 'You never say you love me', looked even more beautiful than the first, the letters were full and plump, with ornate swirls. The final 'e' was smudged and Oliver hoped that this was the splash of a tear as she realised what she was doing.

Had he ever told her he loved her? No, he hadn't. Do actions speak louder than words? Yes, they do. He'd left everything he knew, everyone he loved, to come to live with her in a place where in winter time it was so cold that when you breathed your nostril hairs froze and your eyelids stuck together, where minus fifteen was nothing special and rolling naked in the snow was considered fun.

'You're really happy to give all this up?' she said, after a gig at a pub in Brixton.

'Are you taking the piss?'

'I know how much you love your music.'

'What, can't I play in Helsinki? You never know. I might become massive.'

She brushed a wisp of vanilla-blonde hair from her eyes and grabbed his hand. 'You never know, you just might.'

His band members were neither as charitable nor optimistic. They told him he was an idiot, and out of order. And when that didn't make a difference, they told him they had something good going. But gigs in pubs and vague promises of bigger venues and tours, weren't as good as Sanna. Not even close. Actions, he thought, spoke louder than words. Clearly he was wrong.

He opened the small velvet box sitting on the table beside the note. The ring had six small diamonds, clumped together like a flower. Not flashy, but sophisticated.

Duck and love he could do. No problem. Reason three was tougher.

'You hate the nature'.

That was an exaggeration. He remembered when they arrived. Summer days in her parents' cottage in the forest that just went on and on and on. Sanna, her hair tied back in a bun, wearing nothing but a yellow bikini and red nail varnish as she rowed him to the fish traps. Him lying back and admiring her tanned thighs, the big sky and the ripples on the lake, the sound of the boat splashing and the birds calling.

'This is fantastic,' he said. 'I could write some amazing music here.'

'Is that before or after you kill the fish?'

'What?' He sat up so quick the boat rocked. 'You know I can't…'

She laughed and flicked water at him with her oar. 'Oh, you're such a delicate flower sometimes.'

But she'd taught him how to gut a perch anyway, and even though the smell stayed on his fingers and the scales stuck to his skin, he was secretly proud of himself as he fried the tiny fillets in butter. None of his friends would believe that he was living off the land.

Still it was true, he didn't like the forest work. The chopping down of trees seemingly for the sake of it, the obsession with blueberry and mushroom picking. Sanna's dad's look, half frown, half sneer, when Oliver complained that carrying logs might damage his playing fingers, made him want to skulk away.

Sanna liked to walk for the sake of walking. She liked to row in the rain. She liked to swim naked in the lake in the middle of the night. She was a forest nymph. He was a city boy. He could change, though. He might never love the wilderness like her, but he could hide it better. It was a small price to pay.

Reason four was not.

'You live like a hermit'.

This hurt him more than he'd imagined. Sanna's English was flawless. She knew what a hermit was. Did she know though that when he pictured a hermit, he saw a dirty, stinking, bearded skeleton of a man, babbling and drooling?

Grasping the list, Oliver shuffled to the bathroom and looked in the mirror. His T-shirt was stained with beer. He sniffed under his arms and winced. His beard was scragglier than when they lived in London. There he'd cultivated it, a trim here, a snip there. He was a composer after all, even if his most famous compositions were jingles for dog food and aftershave.

Clients expected music men to look a certain way and he did his best to accommodate. The women seemed to appreciate it, too. And before Sanna there'd been plenty of those. That sharp hipster look had gone to pot in the year he'd been in the Land of the Long Dark. What was the point of worrying about it? He didn't see anyone because nobody wanted to see him. Now he looked more like the woodsman he so clearly wasn't. If he hadn't felt so bleak inside he'd have laughed at the irony. Instead, he stroked his beard.

'You need to meet some people,' Sanna said. 'That's how you'll get work. It's all about who you know, here. Helsinki's such a small place.'

She was right. He got to know it quickly. It was beautiful. The sea, the trams, the parks, the cafes, the bikes everywhere. Just how a vibrant Nordic capital should be. Clean, and fresh and pure. It seemed so cosmopolitan. Then the winter came and the people changed. They stopped speaking. The silence unnerved him. When he went out with Sanna's friends it made him squirm in his chair and stare at his beer. Made him babble more to fill the void. He imagined them afterwards saying how boring he was. The tedious Englishman who never knew when to shut up.

'God, your paranoia knows no bounds,' Sanna said, sitting on his back massaging his shoulders. 'It's not about you. Finns aren't afraid of silence. We came from the forests. We're used to the quiet. We enjoy it. Not like you English.' She made her fingers into a crucifix. 'Oh no, please not another embarrassing silence. Tell me, Oliver, what's so embarrassing about silence?'

'It's just not very sociable, is it?'

'And the constant stream of noise that pours from English people's mouths is, is it?'

She made some sense. Still, he stopped going out as much. Stopped looking for work. Stopped risking those long, lingering pauses in life, those looks when he just couldn't keep his mouth closed.

He splashed himself with water. It felt good. He rubbed some soap into his beard and shaved. That felt good, too. Despite the darkness under his eyes, he was surprised how much better he looked. He got undressed and had a long, long shower. Nothing like a hermit, he thought, as he threw on some clean clothes. Now it felt like he meant business. Sitting at the table, he grabbed a pen and crossed off reason number four.

Then, his gaze fell on number five and he dropped his head into his hands. It was the one that had sent him bowling to a dark bar on that first night rather than rushing through the city and bringing Sanna back to the apartment.

'You want to fuck my sister'.

The letters were bigger, pressed so hard into the paper that the K had ripped into the pad below. There were three exclamation marks.

Seeing the sentence written like that made Oliver's skin crawl. It implied that he was the instigator. That he was the one who'd

78

pranced into the sauna, and made a big show of soaping his body. Yet there was no point lying to himself. Pre-Sanna, he might have tried his luck with her sister. If he was honest, once or twice she'd even invaded his dreams.

'You dream of being the next Bowie as well,' he said to the ceiling. 'That doesn't mean you are.'

It turned his insides to remember that evening. He'd never liked the sauna. It was dark and dry and hot. It made him think of ovens and always left him feeling as though his skin had been broiled.

'That's how it's meant to feel,' Sanna said the first time he complained. 'It's called getting clean.'

'Clean.' Oliver touched his red cheeks. 'This isn't clean. This is scorchio.'

Sanna laughed. 'A hundred years ago women gave birth in places like this.' She threw water on the stones. They hissed and sizzled, sending a cloud of stinging steam into Oliver's face.

As time passed he learnt to cup his hands over his mouth and breathe when the steam came. He learnt it was hotter on the top bench and that the tips of your fingers burnt easiest. He learnt that when all the family visited, everyone went to sauna together.

For Sanna and her family getting naked was as natural as breathing. Oliver wished he was so comfortable, but he was from a strictly non-nudist family. So instead, he averted his eyes. He had no desire to know his potential parents-in-law so intimately. He was sure Sanna's little sister, Meri, enjoyed his discomfort and got off on teasing him with her tennis-coach body. Never crossing her legs, always sticking out her chest. Bending over to pick up the buckets of water. He lost count of the times he had to look at his nails to stop a twitching in his groin.

It didn't help that Sanna insisted on screwing in the sauna. So much so that eventually she only had to say, 'Shall we have a sauna?' for him to get aroused.

'What's changed since King's Cross?' Oliver said once, after a session.

79

'What do you mean?' Sanna said.

'You once told me how happy you were when you first saw all those neon sauna signs there. A little piece of home, you said, until you discovered they were brothels. Then when I asked what was wrong with that, you said a sauna is for having a sauna, not for screwing in.'

Sanna hugged her knees. 'Oh, I don't know. Perhaps London corrupted me. Or perhaps it's always been such an innocent place that I get off on the idea of being dirty here.' She grinned. 'Plus, you don't have to bother with the hassle of getting undressed.'

Remembering those words made Oliver miss her more than ever. But was it his fault the family sauna felt like a sex den? Or that he and Meri were left alone together? Or that she decided to soap herself like some porn star right in front of him? Was it his fault he had a badly hidden hard-on when Sanna walked back in with a beer?

Thinking of her expression when she saw him crouched there, gazing at Meri, made him blush again. The memory of her storming out made him want to curl up on the sofa and chug beer all night long. He hated himself and he'd never hated himself before. He took out the song he'd written for her. The song he was going to sing before he asked her to marry him. The paper was crumpled from when he'd thrown it in the bin. It was called 'In the Sun' and he thought it was the best thing he'd ever written.

He could like her ducks. He could tell her he loved her, because he did so much it hurt. He could try harder to be an outdoorsy type of guy. He could get out more, make a real effort to find a job and learn the language. He could, he was sure, even persuade her he didn't want to fuck her sister. He could do all those things, yet even if he changed, he'd always know inside he was a fraud, pretending to be something he wasn't. Looking at his song about them together, at his piano-less apartment and at the snow covering the dark world outside, he realised even if he could live with the pretence there was one thing he couldn't live with. And that was Finland.

Every one of her reasons for leaving was a direct consequence of moving to this strange country. Even the ducks, which had never taken over their flat in London, had suddenly multiplied when they arrived. If they had stayed in London, he'd doubtless have told Sanna he loved her eventually. He'd would've had to, to keep her there. If they had stayed in London, he wouldn't have to pretend to get off on forests, or adore killing fish or hacking down harmless trees. He could have carried on talking bullshit without worrying and he'd never have been caught in a sauna ogling Sanna's little sister. He walked to the window and yanked it open. He ignored the wind and the snowflakes stinging his face, and shouted with all his being. 'Thanks for nothing, Finland!'

A woman across the road looked in his direction for a second before trudging on, otherwise nothing changed. Finland was still the same. It would always be the same. Oliver looked at the song he still held in his hand. Snowflakes settled on the paper, smudging the ink, melting his words. Sanna would never leave here. She loved it too much.

He took the song and tossed it out the window, watching it drift down onto the street below. It settled on the pavement, in a pool of soft orange neon. He stared at it until it was covered with flakes. Then, head bowed, he walked back into their old bedroom to finish packing.

Lola's Chair

It's Monday afternoon and it's raining. Another grey day in a long line of grey days that seem to have been queuing up for weeks. I'm wondering whether to sneak off to my work den for a quick cup of coffee when, outside the entrance to Victoria Flats, I see a yellow skip piled high with a mishmash of household junk. I run over, have a quick look around and get stuck in. It's not until I've pushed aside some soggy books and a pair of ripped lampshades that I see a lovely burnished birchwood dining chair. It's Edwardian with a beautiful design, delicately carved legs and workmanship that makes my hairs stand on end. I run my fingers over the varnish and smile.

'You're a real stunner, aren't you,' I whisper, picking it up and placing it on the pavement. Just as I'm thinking how to get it to the den without any of the residents spotting me, I hear footsteps.

'What do you think you're doing, son?'

Vernon. His shirtsleeves are rolled up showing off tattoos he's assured me were once rainbow-coloured dragons breathing the words, 'Vernon Lives for Loving'. Now, they're blue grey smudges on old white skin.

'Messing around with rubbish again, are we?' The rolled-up cigarette hanging from his mouth jigs around with his words. He nods at the chair.

I kick a stone into the gutter. 'It's only going to be thrown away.'

'I don't care if it'll be shot into orbit. You don't go through other people's stuff in work time. Understand me?'

I bite my lip and feel the blushing coming on. I breathe deep to try to stop it, but the heat feels like a slap on the cheek. I think of Lola, of the day she called me her passion fruit. Said she liked it when I got so hot.

I nod and take another deep breath.

'Thank the Lord. Now, Mrs Albright in number fifty-seven has a blocked sink. If it's not too much trouble, I'd like you to sort it out.'

The skip will probably be picked up at five, which gives me just over an hour to come back for the chair. I jog into the courtyard and make for Rosemary House. It's a six-storey block of flats, not a house, but it is greenish like the herb. I once pointed out to Lola how the blue balconies that run parallel to each other look like the vertebrae on a giant's spine. She laughed and told me I had a poet's eye and I should write things like that down. So I did, every single observation in a pocket-sized pad I got from the Co-op. I gave it to her on our first anniversary, along with a dozen red roses and a book on antique restoration. She read the pad slowly from cover to cover, then told me how much she loved me. What I'd give to hear her say that again.

Just as I walk in the hallway the sun makes an appearance and turns the air into a cauldron of swirling dust motes. I like the sound of that, so I chant, 'A cauldron of swirling dust motes' as I run up the stairs. Once Lola's back, I'll start a new pad and I'll make that my very first entry. Mrs Albright's flat is on the top floor. By the time I bang on her door, my chanting has turned to gasping. I wonder if she thinks I'm some heavy breather, because it takes a while before the locks clunk open and a small face with a big bush of bluey grey hair appears.

'Took your time,' she says. 'All those stairs, I suppose. Thank those fine fellows at the council. Never listen. Do you know how many stairs I have to climb up?'

'One hundred and twenty-six.'

'You're sharper than you look, dear. Now let's see if you can use that brain of yours to fix my blessed sink.'

I get to work as fast as I can. The sink is blocked solid and it takes longer than normal for the plunger to do the job, but eventually the drain gurgles and spews stinky black water.

'All done.'

'That was quick. You'll make someone a very good husband one day,' Mrs Albright says looking me up and down as if measuring me for my wedding suit.

'That's what I thought, but Lola says I'm too intense. She says I come on too strong all the time.'

'Nothing wrong with a bit of fire in the belly, but mind it doesn't burn you out. Take my Frank, bless him, he couldn't even put a bulb in, but such a passionate fool. Every Friday for thirty-six years he got me a present. Even when he got his dickie heart and Dr Wallis told him to stay in bed, off he'd trot, up and down those damn stairs. Did for him in the end. Found him dead on the fourth floor landing, holding my last present.' She walks over to the mantelpiece and picks up a porcelain basset hound. 'I keep him here in pride of place.'

'I'm sorry to hear about your husband. I'm getting Lola a chair. She loves chairs. She says they are an amazing marriage of function and beauty. She is searching for the perfect form.'

'A practical present from a practical man. She could do a lot worse. Now, let me get you a tea and a chocolate biccy as a thank you.'

'Sorry, I haven't got time now. I've got a really important job to do before five.'

'If you want to get to my age you should learn to slow down,' she says, giving my hand a little squeeze.

Once on the landing, I check outside. Vernon's van is still parked beside the skip. I need to kill some time before he leaves, so I amble down the stairs thinking of Mrs Albright's husband and trying to work out how many Fridays there are in thirty-six years. By the time I get to the ground floor, I reckon there are one thousand eight hundred and seventy two, which is a hell of a lot of presents.

Rather than risk going outside, I carry on walking down into the cellar until I reach my den. It smells of mould and varnish. I look at the rows of chairs lined up and try to imagine how much room you'd need for nearly two thousand, and sit down in an old cherrywood Windsor sackback rocker. 'Shame Lola never got to see you.'

After enjoying the silence for a while, I pull a bag from the shelf. I keep Lola's old black bobble hat inside, so I have a little something of her at work. The day she bought it was so chilly that each time she spoke, her words came out with little puffs of breath. When I told her she looked like my gran, she giggled and smacked me with her handbag. That was three months, two weeks and four days ago. I bury my face in the hat to breathe her, but it doesn't smell of Lola, it smells of dust. Pulling it low over my face, I put on my battered sheepskin jacket hoping that if Vernon's still there he won't notice it's me.

The sky is watery dark. I count twelve streetlamps standing like guards, their fizzy light making the skip shine. I amble towards it with my head down, listening out for Vernon's voice. Lola's chair has been dumped on top of the pile. I move at a trot and, fast as I can, yank it free.

Mrs Albright emerges from the courtyard and waddles closer. 'Is that you? Blimey, I hope this isn't the chair you plan on giving your lady friend.'

'What's wrong with it?'

'You can't use that old thing to woo a lady.'

'I know what Lola likes.'

She tugs my sleeve. 'No woman would want that in her parlour. Why don't you get her something new?'

I feel my face turning red and want to tell her to leave me alone and get out of my way. I want to tell her that I know better than anyone what Lola likes, because I love her. But I don't. I say nothing. I just walk away, hugging the chair. Only when I get to the end of the street, do I look over my shoulder. Mrs Albright is still there, but now she's nothing more than a shadow in the twilight.

It takes me nearly half an hour to walk home. Every time I

hear a car, I think it's Vernon. By the time I arrive, I'm sticky with sweat. I make my way through the brushes and pots of varnish scattered on the living room floor, and place the chair in the centre of the room.

'I bet her husband would've understood,' I say to myself. 'I bet he'd have done the same.'

This chair is the one. I just know it. I feel so pleased that I hug myself. I know it's only me hugging me, but it still feels good. I carry on, squeezing harder. Then I close my eyes and imagine it's her. That's when the doorbell goes. It's so long since I've heard that sound that I stay frozen for a few seconds. Smoothing down my hair, just in case, I run to the door. My hand trembles when I open it.

'Evening, son. Expecting someone else?' Vernon says.

I shrug.

'Knocked off early today, did we?'

I shrug again.

'I just got a call from a concerned resident.'

'Who?'

'Mrs bloody Albright, that's who. She said you'd been acting a bit funny and wanted to make sure you were all right. Mentioned something about a chair.'

'I don't care. I'm doing it for Lola.'

Vernon shakes his head. 'You'll get banged away if you keep this up. You should forget about her and forget about chairs, I'll tell you that for nothing.'

'I can't.'

'Then you're more of a fool than you look.' He crosses his arms. 'This is the last time I'm covering for you. You hear?'

I look at my feet and nod.

'Good. Now I'm off home. Don't be late tomorrow.'

Once he has driven away, I close the door and get my toolbox. Sitting cross-legged on the floor, I sandpaper off the scratched varnish on the smooth curve of the chair leg. I carry on until my arm throbs, then I re-varnish the legs in slow careful strokes, smiling when the colour seeps back into wood. Once they're all done, I march into the kitchen and pick up the phone. I take a deep breath and dial her number. There are nineteen rings before anyone answers.

'Hello.'

'Lola, it's me. It's Robbie.'

'Why do you keep doing this?'

'What?'

'Don't play dumb with me. You know what.'

I feel the blushes blistering my cheeks. 'I've got a dining chair for you. I think it's Edwardian. Birch with a cherry veneer. It had a couple of scratches, but I've fixed them up for you. You'll love it. I know you will.'

'How many chairs have you got me in the last three months?'

I bite my nail. 'Eleven.'

'And how many times have I come over to see them?'

'I've tried so hard to find one you'd like and you don't even come and look. Please, Lola, the least you can do is see it for yourself.'

A click and the phone starts purring.

'Lola?'

I stare at the receiver, willing her voice to come back. But when willing doesn't work, I go back into the living room and sit on chair number twelve. It feels good, solid and comfortable, smooth yet sturdy. I sit there for a long time, eyes closed, thinking. I decide I'll keep this chair in the house.

Mind made up, I smile and start calculating how many chairs I'd find Lola in thirty-six years. Not that I'm going to search that long. Course not. One more, that's all. It's got to be worth a try, hasn't it. Lucky number thirteen might just be the one she can't resist. It might just be Lola's chair.

Estrella and the Gringo

Estrella was shelling peas in the courtyard when Aunty shouted at her to come and say hello. Merengue blasted from Radio Panamericana, so she pretended not to hear, sure that it would be the padre or one of Aunty's stupid friends. But when she looked up she saw it was a young gringo. She was so surprised she knocked the bowl over, spilling peas across the concrete.

'Sorry, I don't normally have that effect on people,' he said in Spanish, looking at her the same way Alejandro had the day they first meet.

He said his name was Doug. Up closer, she could see he was older than she first thought. Twenty-five at least. Perhaps more. He had messy maize-coloured hair, and a nose that took up too much room. His mouth was pretty though, like a girl's, and his eyes were river green. A gold stud glinted in his eyebrow. He touched it when he saw her staring.

'I got it in Rio. It seemed like a good idea at the time.'

'I think it suits you,' Aunty said, putting a painted fingernail to her lip.

It was then Estrella realised that Aunty had curled her hair and put on the yellow blouse she normally kept for the padre's visits. Perfume too. Aunty had known the gringo was coming, yet hadn't said a word.

'I've never seen a man wear gold like that. Is it a gringo thing?'

Aunty patted her on the head as if she were a dog. 'Oh, don't mind this one, Señor. Estrella may be nineteen, but she still has plenty to learn about manners.' She grabbed Doug's elbow. 'Now, your room is ready. I've made it up especially for you.'

'Thanks,' he said. 'You're very kind.'

Estrella watched Aunty flutter her eyelashes, as if Doug had told her she was most beautiful woman in the world. He didn't notice.

He was too busy looking around the courtyard. 'Your flowers are amazing.'

'They're my babies. I treat them well and they keep me happy with their colour.'

Estrella rolled her eyes. It was true, the yellow angel's trumpets with a fragrance that gave you strange dreams, the cantutas, and the purple orchids stuffed in old paint pots, were beautiful. But if they were Aunty's babies, why in the Virgin's name was it her who watered them every morning and every night?

'Give me a little while and I can show you around our town,' Aunty said, pushing her bosom out.

'That's okay. Once I've dumped my gear, I can check it out myself.'

'I need to buy some bread,' Estrella said. 'I'll come with you.'

Aunty's mouth puckered up like a dried plum, but she didn't say a word. She didn't have to. Estrella knew what she was thinking.

While Aunty showed Doug his room, Estrella counted on her fingers how many gringos she'd seen in her life. She could remember seven. Three missionaries. Two doctors. One NGO man and a tourist who came through town once on a motorbike. She wondered why this one had come.

When Doug returned, he'd changed into army shorts and a T-shirt that said 'Born to Surf'. A big camera hung around his neck.

'Ready?' Estrella asked.

'I'm always ready,' he said.

She led him through the courtyard and out into the street. A *campesino* was herding his goats, making dust rise into the air like mud-coloured fog. Doug pointed his camera at them. 'Damn, this place is cool.'

'You think? Surely goats are goats everywhere?'

'Yeah, but you don't see them wandering down the street where I'm from.'

As they walked, he turned his head this way and that as though

94

he was looking at the world for the first time. When they got to the plaza and he saw the statue of Bolívar riding his horse, he clapped his hands together.

'Bet he's a hero round here, right?'

'Who?'

'Bolívar.'

Estrella laughed. 'Don't be stupid. He's been dead over a hundred years.'

Doug got on his knees and started snapping again. 'I've read all about him. Not many people who've freed a whole continent, hey? Just shows you can do worthwhile stuff when you travel.'

'I wouldn't know. I've never been anywhere.'

'I'm going to teach English in the countryside. My dad says I'm a bum just travelling around, so I'm going to show him different.' He spun round, taking pictures of the church, the mountains, even Don Miguel sprawled on a bench.

It was funny seeing how people reacted to him. *Mamitas* held their knitting still, men froze, cigarettes hanging from their lips. Kids stopped their games and giggled. When some boys Estrella used to play football with pouted and made kiss-kiss sounds, she blew kisses right back.

Yet despite the looks, and the way words chased each other out of his mouth, Estrella enjoyed his chatter. He was full of energy, like a child after too much cake. She was listening so carefully she didn't notice the padre until he squeezed her shoulder.

'And who have we here, young lady?' he said.

'Why don't you ask him yourself? He speaks Spanish.'

Even though the padre's sunglasses covered his eyes, Estrella knew he was looking down her top. He stroked the scar on his chin. The one he said he got in the service of Christ, but that Estrella knew was really from falling off his motorbike, drunk.

He took Doug's hand in both of his. 'We're always happy to see new faces in our little town. Will you be staying long?'

'Few weeks, maybe. Not really sure yet.'

95

The padre ran his hands through his gelled hair. 'My church is there. You're always welcome.'

Estrella tugged Doug's elbow. 'We have to go.'

He paused for a second, then followed her across the plaza. 'You got a problem with him?'

Estrella wanted to say that the padre was a son of a bitch hypocrite. That after fat Gloria had caught her with Alejandro in the forest, the padre had preached about the whores of Babylon leading good people down the road to ruin. And that two nights later, she saw him kissing Aunty in the moonlight and that the bastard came around her house all the time now. But she didn't have the guts, so she ignored the question and instead asked Doug if he wanted to take her picture.

Doug took the *colectivo* bus into the countryside the next morning. When he saluted Estrella from the window, she waved back, ignoring the gawping *campesinos* and the kids pushing their faces against the dusty glass.

It was two days later before she saw him again. She'd just got back from the market, and was weighed down with *granadillas*, *cherimoyas* and maize. It wasn't just her shoulders that ached. Her head hurt, too. It was tiring ignoring the sniggers and the whistles, the whispers and the stares, especially when Aunty said it was exactly what she deserved for spreading her legs for a travelling salesman.

If Estrella had known then about Aunty and the padre, she wouldn't have bitten her lip when Aunty said she was a slut just like her mama. Instead, she would've told her that she might be all high and mighty on the outside, but inside she was no better than Estrella. Worse even, because the padre was meant to save his love for God, not for a woman like her.

Papi would have stood by her. He hated his older sister almost as much as she did.

'It won't be for long, Princess. Promise,' he said, on the steps of the bus. 'And when I come back we'll get a new place together, far away from you know who.'

It might have been nearly two years, but she still remembered the sound of his laugh when he said it. The memory must have made her look sad, because when she walked into the courtyard Doug jumped up as fast as a cricket and rushed over.

'What's the matter with you?' He grabbed the bags. 'Let me take those before your arms fall off.'

'You're back already?'

He nodded at the *granadillas*. 'Can I have an orange?'

'That's no orange, stupid!'

'Well, it sure looks like one.'

'Try to peel it then.'

He did as he was told. The peel cracked and white fluff puffed out.

'What's that?'

'Pull the skin off and have a look.'

He worked his fingers over the surface. When he saw the slimy green insides, his face screwed up as if he'd just opened a parcel of pig liver. 'I'm not eating that. It looks like something you cough up when you're ill.'

Estrella laughed. 'That makes you a coward.'

'I'm no coward. Watch.' He threw back his head and gulped the green jelly. 'Wow, that tastes fantastic!'

'See, bravery has its rewards.'

Aunty leant out the window, her hair in curlers. 'Estella, where have you been hiding yourself? The toilet needs scrubbing, and I've got Señora Lida coming over for a *cafecito*. Get to it, girl.'

'Why don't you get to it yourself?'

'By all the saints, I don't need your lip. I give you a roof over your head and you talk to me like I'm nothing. You know where the door is if you're not happy.' Her face froze. 'Oh, Doug, I didn't see you there! I'm just making some lunch. You'll eat with me, won't you? I want to hear all about your time in the countryside.'

'Is your Aunty always like that to you?' he whispered behind his hand.

'Like what?'

'A stupid witch.'

Estrella giggled. 'Yes. Nearly always.'

When Aunty reappeared she looked like someone out of a Colombian soap opera. Doug stared at her, just like all the men did whenever Aunty dressed up special.

'Come, Doug. I want to hear all your stories. Did the *campesinos* disturb you? Isn't it terrible how they live?'

Doug followed her into the kitchen. A hungry puppy after a bone. When Estrella heard them laughing together, she put her fingers in her ears and sung.

A few days later, Doug caught up with Estrella while she was walking to the park. Although Estrella didn't have time to play football anymore, she still liked to go there to watch the kids play. It reminded her of the days before Papi had left.

'Guess who?' Doug said, putting his hands over her eyes.

'The President of the Republic?'

'If only. Where you going?'

'To the forest. Want to come?'

She took him the same way she went with Alejandro, but this time she made sure they walked further from the path. Maybe he knew what she wanted, but he didn't say anything. They sat by the river for a while, listening to the birds and the crickets.

'You have pretty fingers,' she said eventually.

'You think?'

She took his hand. 'They are soft too. Like baby skin.'

He laughed. 'Don't tell my dad. He thinks I've never done a hard day's work in my life.'

'You always talk about your papa.'

'Do I?'

'Yes. Do you miss him?'

98

'You must be joking.'

'Is he handsome?'

He threw a stone in the river. 'If you like bald men with glasses.'

'Do you think Aunty is pretty?'

'Yeah, for an older woman.'

'She wants you.'

'What do you mean?'

'As her lover.'

'What?' He laughed. 'Don't be stupid. She's just being friendly.'

'I know her and she's after you. She thinks because you're a gringo you're rich.' She edged closer. 'Have you ever kissed a Peruvian girl?'

He arched his back and cracked his knuckles. 'Oh man, if this is going where I think it's going, we should probably be heading back.'

'Is it that you want Aunty or are you just too scared to try? Like you were with the *granadillas*?'

He blinked and licked his lips. 'No! I'm not scared. It's just I came here to do something worthwhile, not to party.'

She caressed his neck. 'I think you're scared.'

'Yeah?'

'Yes.'

He grabbed her face and kissed her hard. His mouth tasted of mint and cigarettes. He pushed his tongue deeper than Alejandro had and Estrella remembered what they said about all gringo girls being easy. Even though she didn't like his smoky taste, she made sure she didn't pull away.

After that, whenever he was back from the countryside, he tried to find ways to be alone with her. Even when Aunty was in the same room, he'd squeeze Estrella's elbow or bang into her and pretend it was an accident. Aunty was too caught up in her own head to realise anything. She still made Doug take lunch with her and still dressed herself up like a soap star.

The padre suspected her of something, though. He may have been a sleaze, but he was no donkey brain. One Monday, he stopped Estrella in the plaza and asked how much longer the gringo was staying.

'Why do you want to know?'

'I'm curious, that's all.' He smiled with his too-white teeth.

'Worried he'll take your place?'

'What are you talking about, girl?'

'You know.'

His smiled stayed fixed, but his nostrils flared like an angry horse's. 'Do you think anyone will listen to a word that comes from your filthy mouth? You ooze sin from every pore just like your mama. I'm counseling your aunty. Helping her deal with the sadness you have brought her. Understand?'

Estrella laughed. 'Counseling wasn't what the boys at school called what you and Aunty do.'

'You are going straight to hell, Estrella Vargas, as surely as night follows day.'

The way he marched away, chest out, arms swinging like a soldier's, she knew she had got to him. The thought kept her singing all afternoon.

A couple of weeks later, while she was feeding the chickens, Doug told her that Aunty had asked him if he thought she was beautiful.

'And?' Estrella said, tossing grain in big handfuls.

'I said yes of course.'

She spun round and threw chicken feed at him.

'Hey, what are you doing?' he said, flapping like one of the birds.

'You've never told me I'm beautiful.'

'Well, course you are. Beauty runs in your family. And you are, you're really beautiful.'

She let him kiss her then, but she could tell by the way he pressed himself hard against her that he wanted more. When she pushed him off, he said something in English and kicked the wall.

'Damn it. I'm leaving.'

'What! Why? Because I don't let you kiss me when I'm feeding chickens?'

He crossed his arms. 'No, because your aunty is trying to get into my pants. And because you won't let me touch you.'

'What about trying to prove to your papa that you can do something worthwhile with your life?'

'I've been here long enough,' he said. 'I've emailed him the photos. I've shown him I'm no waster.'

'If you go I want to come with you.'

'Don't be ridiculous, Estrella. You live here.'

'I don't want to live here anymore.'

He sighed. 'I can't take you with me. I'm travelling around South America until my cash runs out and then I'm going home.'

'You're just like my papi.'

'What do you mean?'

'You run away from your problems.'

'Listen, I don't need this, okay. You're a sweet girl, but I was never going to stay forever. And now your aunty is going all weird, it's time to leave.'

'If that's how you see things, I want to give you something to remember me by.'

'You do?'

She sat on his lap, and stroked his face. 'Yes I do.'

'When?'

'Meet me in the plaza just before noon.'

'You've got a date,' he said grinning.

The rest of the morning Estrella praised herself for keeping calm. When she'd wanted to slap Doug's selfish face, she'd caressed it. When she wanted to kick him between the legs, she'd sat on his lap. Just like everyone else, he said one thing and did another. If he'd come to her town to help people, what was wrong with helping her? If he had money to travel around South America, he had money to take her with him. She practised looking happy in front of the mirror before she went to meet him in the plaza, but her smile looked as fake as a plastic doll's.

He was waiting besides Old Sergio's ice cream trolley, playing with two *campesina* girls. Their ponytails, like black rope, swung back and forth as he chased them in circles. He was good with kids. One day, he might make a good husband and father to someone. Estrella took a deep breath, kissed the ring Papi left her and marched over.

'Hey there,' he said, breathless. 'These two are in my class.' He nodded at the girls.

She smiled at them and took his hand. 'Let's go. I haven't got much time.'

'Where to?'

'Put your arm around me.'

'Here?'

'Yes, here. You're leaving, no? What does it matter who sees us now?'

He shrugged and wrapped his arm around her shoulders. It felt good even when she saw mamitas nudge each other and point and the girls run to get their friends. Estrella marched them towards the doors of the church just as the bell struck. Once she'd counted the twelve chimes, she grabbed Doug's face and kissed him.

She teased him with her tongue, imagining they were dancing at a fiesta. Over his shoulder, she saw the church doors open. The padre strode out, sunglasses in his hand, squinting in the midday sun. When he saw them, he pulled his hands up to shield his face and stared.

'Whoah! You're eager,' Doug said, licking his lips.

'This what you wanted, isn't it?' She glared at the padre. Even though his face was now in shadow, she saw his too-white teeth and his frown. She waited for him to say something, but he just carried on looking. He was still staring when she took Doug's hand and led him to the forest path.

The patio was quiet when they returned a couple of hours later. It felt as if the house was holding its breath. No dogs, no radio, no Aunty singing. The only sounds came from outside. A cow's sad bellowing, beeping motorbike horns.

Then a door slammed. 'Estrella, is that you, girl?'

She didn't say anything.

Doug let go of her hand and stopped grinning. 'What's gotten into her?'

Before she could answer, Aunty burst out of the kitchen. She was breathing hard. Her hair was messed up like she'd been in a storm and her hands were clenched. The padre stood behind her, shaking his head.

'Is it true what the padre tells me?' Aunty hissed. 'You've been whoring yourself in the forest again.'

She felt her face flush. 'The padre should know. He's an expert on whores.'

Aunty took two quick steps and slapped her so hard it felt as if her cheek had been whipped with nettles.

'I want you out of my house.' She glared at Doug. 'I want you both out of my house.'

Estrella rubbed her face and felt tears coming. It wasn't from the pain or because the padre was smirking and pulling Aunty close like he cared. It was the way Doug looked at her.

'I'd rather be a whore than a hypocrite,' she shouted so loud the dogs began barking.

'Get out, Estrella, and take your gringo with you.'

She dragged Doug upstairs. He sat on his bed, head in his hands. 'All we did was go for a walk. What's her problem?'

'She listens to the wrong people.'

'Is she really getting it on with the padre?'

Estrella nodded.

'That's crazy.' He sighed. 'Suppose I better get packing. What are you going to do?'

'I'm coming with you.'

Doug looked at his nails. 'Surely there's somewhere else you can go?'

'No.' She grabbed his shoulders. 'You want to help people, help me.'

'That's different, Estrella.'

'Why?'

He got up and dragged his rucksack from under the bed. 'It just is.'

'I will have to go to the brothel then.'

'What! Are you serious?'

'Nobody else will give me work. It's that or begging.'

Doug mumbled something in English. 'Hurry up then. I want to get out of here as quick as I can.'

She went to hug him, but he pushed her away. 'You can thank me later.'

Estrella didn't say anything in the taxi to the bus station. Her heart was thumping so hard she was sure she would choke if she spoke. When the taxi driver asked where they were off to Doug said wherever the first bus was going. She hoped it was Cusco. That was where Papi had last been seen.

They got the last two seats on a bus to Abancay. At least it was going in the right direction. It wasn't until the driver started the engine that Estrella felt tears coming.

'What are you crying for?' Doug wiped the window. 'I thought you hated this place.'

She shrugged. 'I do, but…'

She hoped he'd take her hand. Instead, he pulled on a pair of headphones and turned up his music. It only took a few minutes to drive through the town, past the church and the park. Past her old school and Don Miguel asleep on the bench in the plaza. Past the cake shop Papi used to take her every Friday after football. When it was all behind them, she wiped her face and tried to make herself comfortable. It wasn't easy. The seat was worn, the road potholed and Doug was frowning to his gringo tunes. She stared ahead and saw the bus driver had golden charms and pictures of the Virgin on his dashboard to protect him on the long journey ahead. Clinging to her bag, she closed her eyes and wished for someone to protect her, too.

Burnt

Even though she saw a man on fire as she turned the corner, Cindy didn't stop. She didn't even slow down. People don't just spout flames by the side of the road on a quiet Barrett housing estate. Her hormones must be making her see things.

'Did you see anything strange back there?' she said, after a few seconds.

Melvin yawned. 'What, you mean the fire guy?'

Cindy stared at him. 'You saw him too? Why the hell didn't you say anything?'

'I've got other things on my mind.' He tapped his BlackBerry. 'Annual report's late.'

Cindy stopped the car. The fluffy dice that Melvin had bought her because it was kitsch cool swung back and forth between them. She stroked her belly and tried to send comforting thoughts to its inhabitant.

'I'm going back to see if he's okay. You phone an ambulance or something.'

'We're not the ones to sort this stuff out.'

Cindy did hear him. She had heard him for nearly three years now. Heard him when he told her she was 'magnificent'. Heard him when he said 'I do'. Heard him when, with a grin, he said 'as long as it's perfect I don't care what you call it'. She studied his profile. He was handsome, in a catalogue model, stare-blandly-at-your-watch type way. He had money, and thanks to his I-have-to-work-late job, he always would have. And he'd ignored a burning man.

She spun the car around.

'What are you doing, Cindy?' Melvin grabbed her arm. 'We can't miss this scan.'

At that moment she wished she could run. She wished she

109

could run over hills and through woods, with rain drizzling her face and air sailing down her lungs. She wished she were anywhere other than in the car with Melvin. She yanked herself free.

'I'm going back to see if the man is all right, all right?' she said, accelerating so quickly Melvin was thrown backward into his seat.

He didn't say anything, but brought his hands together in front of his face and puffed his cheeks.

Inside her belly, the baby fluttered. Cindy knew what Melvin was thinking. He was wondering if he'd still have to pay the doctor, wondering if a burning man was a valid excuse, wondering how much longer he'd have to wait to find out if the baby was good enough for him.

An ambulance was parked beside the curb. There was no siren, but its lights were spinning. An old woman and a couple of kids with a spaniel were standing beside it. Melvin sat up. A smirk spread across his face. 'See, Cindy. There is nothing you can do.'

Cindy stared ahead at the paramedics crouched by a smouldering heap. One of them held a charred briefcase. She undid her seat belt and, caressing her bump, glared at Melvin.

'You're wrong. Actually there is something I can do.' She opened the door and clambered outside. 'I can act like a human being.'

'Don't be silly, we'll miss our appointment!'

Cindy ignored him and walked to the ambulance. Looking in she could see the burnt man lying on a gurney, shaking and moaning. It was impossible to tell his age. Half his face was stained black as if with tar; the other half flared rose red. The air smelled like it did that time she caught her fringe in the dinner candles, only much, much worse.

Reaching for the handrails, Cindy gingerly pulled herself into the ambulance and stood by the gurney.

'Coming with us, love?' asked a paramedic.

'Yes.'

'Family?'

'Oh yes.'

At this the man looked at her. They stared at each other a long time.

'Breathe,' Cindy said. 'You have to keep breathing.'

One Long Queue of Zeros

Jemima's craving the young American. It's obvious by the way her gaze skips across the others like a hungry bird hopping from one bare branch to another. When her eyes rest on Megan Bloom, Jemima doesn't blink. Instead, she swallows as if gulping down the girl's luminosity. Out of all the applicants, this one's the brightest. She has the brightest hair, the brightest smile, the brightest eyes, the brightest brain.

'We're a diamond of a company. Investment banking alone pulls in enough to make the GDP of a small country look like chump change.' The skin on Jemima's rawboned face is pulled tighter by her leer. 'We've got people battering down the door for a shot at working here.'

While the other candidates squirm or sit bolt upright, Megan lounges as if her chair is as comfy as a beanbag.

'Think you've got what it takes?' Jemima continues.

They all bob their heads in unison, a chorus line of nodding dogs. Jemima looks at me, challenging me to challenge her.

'A diamond of a company indeed.' I clap my hands. The applicants jump. 'But are diamonds really forever?'

The two men, boys really, fresh from university, one with a suit so new he's forgotten to take the tag off, glance at each other. The prickly girl with the razor cheekbones and a Home Counties accent nods as if she understands, but only Megan Bloom scribbles a note.

Jemima smacks her pad and jerks her pen back like a knife thrower. I've made her hundreds of thousands in bonuses. Numbers that end with one long queue of zeros. She hates me for it. She hates me because she knows I get away with whatever I want.

'Why don't you just fuck off to Goa or somewhere equally

tie-dye if you think this job is so morally redundant?' she said to me after I'd dissuaded my first applicant.

'I'd like to pay the company back before I leave.'

'For what?'

'For ninety-hour weeks. For a wife who walked out. For making me greedy.'

'Oh please!'

I point at the boy with the tag hanging off his collar. 'Are you ready to sacrifice your life to make rich people richer?'

'You bet I am. I'm ready to start right now.' He blushes, and I feel sorry for him because it is so clear that he will always be disappointed in his aspirations.

Jemima sighs loudly. Everyone but Megan turns to look. I flash my pad at her. Written in big bold letters are the words THIS JOB SUCKS.

She gasps and clamps her hand over her mouth. Jemima whips her head around and shoots me with an Uzi glare. 'Did you say something?'

'No, not a word.'

But Jemima can see that I intrigue the young American. For the rest of the meeting, the girl focuses her attention on my every word. After a few more of Jemima's questions and one stifled yawn from me, we say our goodbyes.

Jemima tries to herd them out, but Megan is fast on her feet. As I walk back onto the trading floor to immerse myself in the barking barrage of orders, she rushes up to me and says, 'You were kidding around with me, right? You know, with the sign and all?'

I shake my head.

'Is this one of those psychological tests?'

Just as I'm about to reply, Jemima calls her over. I watch them standing together in reception, a lusterless woman and a luminous girl. That's your future, I want to shout, but the door closes and she is gone.

Two days later I get an email on my Nokia from Jemima. She

says Megan Bloom declined her offer of a second interview. She says it's my fault. She says I'm a fucking liability. Before pressing delete, I enjoy the feeling, a sensual mix of relief and triumph, which washes over me on these occasions. It doesn't last. It never does. There are so many more willing to take Megan Bloom's place. Nonetheless, when I see my reflection, superimposed upon the red and green numbers tricking down my trading screen, I'm still smiling.

The Grounding of Tiffany Hope

As I floated over the backyard, I admired the watery pink of the dawn sky and the way the dew made the grass shine. It gave me goosebumps to feel so light. As if I was made of nothing but feathers and candyfloss. When I reached the fence I did a slow-motion forward roll and kicked off in the opposite direction. I was so lost in the moment, I didn't notice the light come on in Mum's window or see her wrench the curtains apart.

It wasn't until I heard the window rattle open that I dropped barefooted onto the flowerbed. By the time I ran back to the house, she was standing in the kitchen doorway. 'Think you're all clever sneaking up in the morning, do you?' she said.

I shrugged.

She grabbed my shoulders. 'Don't shrug at me, girl. How many times have I told you? Keep your feet on the ground or your life will be a mess!'

'I'm nineteen, Mum. I can make my own mind up.'

She slapped me, only once, but hard. 'Don't you dare give me any of your back talk. If I'd been stronger when I was nineteen, you might still have a dad and I might still have a man and we might not be living in this godforsaken excuse for a town.'

I bit my lip and said nothing.

She stared at me with strained hot eyes. 'I know it's difficult, Tiff, I know how nice it feels. But if you keep doing it, it will screw your head up. Promise me you'll stop.'

I nodded because I wanted to shut her up.

Later, we ate breakfast together like nothing had happened. And all the time I was wondering if I could stop, just like that.

I'd been wondering that exact same thing since I was seven, when one morning Mum sat me down, and asked me to see if I could touch the ceiling. I'd thought she was crazy or playing some game till my wishing made me float off her lap. She grabbed my ankles and yanked me down, cursing. I wanted to try again, but she held me so tight I couldn't breathe. She told me that it was a disease I'd caught off her. All the women in her family had it. It had ruined her life and she wouldn't let it ruin mine. But it wasn't that easy. In fact it was damn difficult, especially when things weren't going too well, which was pretty much always.

She'd only caught me a few times since, but I knew how angry it got her when it happened. For the rest of the week I kept out of her sight. Like always, I had no money, so I spent my time in the town library. In the tall, white quiet of the place I lost myself in travel books. I'd not once been abroad and loved to read about the world beyond our town. If I hadn't been hanging out there I wouldn't have seen the advert for a library helper, and if Mum hadn't caught me floating I wouldn't have filled out an application. I didn't hold out much hope, but I had an interview and got offered the job there and then. Even when my boss, a chubby man with eyebrows like bird's wings, let slip I was the only applicant it didn't stop me walking tall.

Mum didn't believe me at first. Then I showed her my name badge and she pulled me tight and said all I needed now was to get myself a boy and I'd be well on the way to a proper respectable life. She started talking about Dad and if only he'd stuck around to see what a fine girl I'd grown into. I let her do the talking, but I wished she didn't have to sour the day with talk of someone who'd never been anything more to me than tatty snaps and tears.

It was easy work in the library, and often when there wasn't much happening, I'd gaze at the painted angels on the ceiling wondering how they looked close up. Sometimes, on my lunch hour, I'd lie on the grass outside and stare at the sky imagining myself drifting amongst the clouds. I hoped the craving to float would go away, with a proper job, but it carried on tugging at me, like a kite on a string.

I hoped things would get better at home too, but Mum kept going on about how I should get myself a boyfriend. They way she talked you'd think I could just pop down to Sainsbury's and pick one off the shelf.

'Listen, sweetheart. A girl your age should be having fun. Not moping about at home all the time.'

'And you'd know all about that, right?'

'It's different for me.'

She was having one of her crying days when her skin was as thin as newspaper, so I didn't say anything more. But she must have known what I was thinking, because she turned the TV on and gave me the silent treatment for the rest of the afternoon.

I couldn't sleep properly that night and next morning I woke with a head buzzing with guilty thoughts. To cheer myself up, I took a new way into town and stopped off at the shop for something sweet and sticky. I hadn't seen the man behind the counter before. He had a friendly face, round and smiley, and looked at me with pretty, long-lashed eyes. The badge on his overalls said Jordan.

'I've seen you,' he said, 'You work at the library. You stamped my motorbike book once.'

'I don't remember,' I said, blushing. 'I stamp lots of books.'

'You ever wondered how many words there are in that place? Billions, I'd reckon. Probably more words in your place than there are people in the whole world. You ever think about stuff like that?'

'No, not really.'

'Best not to, otherwise you'll get yourself an almighty headache. Some people go crazy with thinking and dreaming too much. I think it's best to stick to what you know, what you can see with your own eyes. Like I can tell you're a pretty girl. I don't need a book to tell me that.'

I didn't know what to say, so I walked out without buying any sweets after all. I ran to work and spent the day wondering if this

123

Jordan with the pretty eyes was teasing me. In the evening, when I got home, Mum was singing along to her Elvis records. 'I could listen to his voice forever,' she said, with her eyes closed.

I watched her swaying to 'Love Me Tender' and wondered who she imagined was holding her in arms. It was such a sad sight that, rather than ask her advice, I ran upstairs to my room and put my music on to drown out hers.

For the next few days I walked to work a different way, but then one morning at breakfast Mum started talking about boyfriends and wasting my life again. Her taunting got me so wound up that I took the path past the shop. When Jordan saw me he hung out the window and waved at me. I ignored him, but smiled all the same.

After that, I started going past the shop more often. It was nice to have someone act so friendly. Often he'd shout out that he was coming to get his book stamped, but I'd look at the pavement and say nothing. Somehow though, he still managed to wiggle himself into my thoughts. At lunchtime when I lay on the grass, I started seeing his face in clouds.

It was a crisp, fresh spring morning, the type that makes you think that your life has started up all new, when he ran out of the shop to say hello.

'Listen, I've been thinking,' he said, grinning. 'I see you practically every day. But I don't even know your name.'

'It's Tiffany. Tiffany Hope.'

'Okay, Tiffany, the reason I wanted to know is because…' He looked at his nails. 'I'd like to take you out. How about tonight?' I thought of Mum's words and said yes.

She gave me a big hug when I told her and spent hours doing my nails and hair. 'You look a real beauty, a proper lady,' she said. 'Be back by ten and make sure you don't do anything silly.'

She didn't say anything else, but we both knew what she meant.

That first night Jordan took me bowling. I was so bad I almost cried, but he said there was no point worrying about it. Some people are good at some things and some people are good at others. I wanted to tell him there and then that I could float, but I bit my lip and nodded. I got back nearer to eleven, but Mum didn't say a thing.

They went fast, those first few months together, but it was still a big shock when Jordan asked me to marry him. It felt too soon, but I still said yes and then had to stop myself from clapping my hand over my mouth. When I told Mum she grabbed hold of me and danced me round the room and told me I was luckier than a lottery winner.

Jordon found us a basement flat. It was exciting at first, getting everything perfect, decorating our little old nest in the ground, but as the weeks turned into months I started feeling heavier. And when I slept, I started to dream of floating again. It was always somewhere different, with elephants or women in funny dresses. Places far away from town and from Jordan. In the morning, I'd wake up sweating and itchy with guilt.

The longer we were together, the more I found out little things about him that got me angry. He talked too much about things he knew nothing about. When I said how I'd like to go on holiday, he'd laugh and say why waste money on that when you can just turn on the Discovery Channel. And he thought because I was a woman I should do everything and he could just lie around reading motorbike magazines. Maybe it wouldn't have been so bad if I could have carried on floating, but by then all I did was hold my slowly swelling belly and wait for the small kicks that came more often than ever.

After little Chloe was born, there were times when Jordan was snoring in our bed, and I was rocking the baby and watching the sun creep through the curtains. I'd go stand by the window and, opening the catch carefully so as not to wake the baby, I'd breathe the cool morning air and wonder what would happen if I just slipped out and away?

I didn't though. How could I? I had Chloe to think about and I had a proper life just like Mum wanted for me. Every time

I saw her she made me make the same promise. Don't you ever do it again, she'd say. Don't throw all this away. Remember your dad. Bolted faster than a whippet when he found out. Then she'd look at Chloe and in a hushed voice say how she prayed every night the curse hadn't been passed onto the little one. I'd nod, but sometimes when I was alone, I'd take Chloe in my arms, rise up real slow from the floor and swim slow laps of the small blue living room. And every time, she would look at me with those big green eyes and smile.

The Sheriff of Love and the Rainbow Girl

Hard work? No, it wasn't really hard work. True, I didn't enjoy trudging streets all day, or so many slammed doors or so much rudeness, but in the end that wasn't what made me stop. Sharing my cards with those less fortunate felt like a special burden, no matter what people said. What changed me wasn't labour measured in miles marched and doors knocked upon, it was meeting the girl and the powerful craving to meet her again.

It began in the library, an old corn exchange with a tall ceiling and sheaves carved over the doorway. Normally I'm not one for libraries, they remind me too much of my dad and his study, but it was raining, plump, drenching drops, and the Queen of Hearts directed me to its shelter. The girl was perched on a table, as if ready to leap off. When I saw her, I froze in mid-step. It was as if my world had been reduced to a circle around her face.

And what a face. Eyes taking up all the space reserved for eyes and more, a cherub nose and lips that seemed in perpetual pout, all embraced by a cloud of honey hair. I wondered if there had ever been a girl more perfectly formed. Even when she frowned at me, I didn't think I'd seen a more beautiful creature in my entire twenty-three years.

'Had a good enough look, have we?' she said. 'Or perhaps I should parade up and down or give you a little spin?'

'Sorry, I didn't mean to, it's just…'

'I'm a girl, you're a boy. You've evolved this way. It's a historical inevitability. You can't help yourself. Listen, I've heard them all and more, so don't even try, all right?'

'I have a feeling you're the one.'

Now it was her turn to stare at me, from top to toe. I wondered what passed through her mind. Did she take my stubble and chaotic curls to be signs of someone unable to look after the very basics of his life, or did she see beyond that to a man unconcerned about the trivialities of appearance. A man living on a higher plane, with more glorious issues at stake.

'You need a haircut.'

'Where do you live?'

'In a world full of nutters.'

'I'm the sheriff of love and the cards have led me to you.'

She laughed. 'Well, cowboy, I'm afraid you've drawn a bad hand, because I'm so far from being the one you can hardly believe.'

'Are you sure?'

She nodded, and it was only then I noticed the rainbow tattooed on her shoulder. Before I could say another word, she strode outside. I gazed at the space she'd inhabited. Then I paced around it, examining it for clues, for a bit of her. I sniffed the air to see if her essence might have lingered. Even when the librarian told me it was early closing, I stayed put. Not until he returned, put one hand on my shoulder and escorted me out, did I move.

'What was that girl's name?'

'You don't want to know, son. Leave it at that. Now out you go. We're open again bright and early tomorrow morning.'

I wandered the streets for the rest of the afternoon. The town was much the same as many others I'd found myself in. Market square, church that looked more like a castle, statues of some long-dead notable holding court from a pedestal. And the people were much the same, too. I watched them traipsing about the town and ferreting around in shops. They sat glum in offices dedicating their lives to acquiring more and more money to buy more and more junk they didn't need, feeling empty and not knowing why. I wondered if this mystery girl felt that way too. I wanted to help show her that there were other options, but I didn't know if I was on the right path. I did what I always did when unsure. I sat down on a bench and pulled out my playing cards.

I emptied the pack into my hand, shuffled them and fanned them out before me. They were getting battered and a few were torn at the edges, but I couldn't replace them. I closed my eyes and picked one. The three of diamonds. I smiled and at that very moment the sunshine came through the cloud and stroked my face. It was clear what I should do. Inspired and with a new sense of purpose, I turned down another street and knocked at number three. A woman opened. A huge, broad-shouldered woman with cropped orange hair and purple painted eyes.

Out of habit, I began my talk, but no, her life didn't lack love or direction. How could it when she had three kids to look after and worked Thursdays and Mondays? If anything, it was bursting with affection and was too predictably direct. In fact, she'd give her right arm for a bit of a change, but if that's what I was selling, I'd come to the wrong place, because all her money, every last penny, went on her kids. That was what being a mum was about, wasn't it?

If I hadn't interrupted her, she might have gone on like that for hours, purging herself of her life, one word at a time. I tried to ask her if the girl was her only daughter, but she submerged me with her noise. Eventually, I just shouted.

'Can I talk to your rainbow girl?'

She rolled her eyes and crossed her arms, squeezing her great breasts together. 'What are you going on about?'

'The pretty girl I just met lives here. The cards told me…'

'I haven't got time for this today. Goodbye.' She slammed the door in my face.

I stood staring at the tear-shaped knocker and slapped my forehead. Silly, silly me, the three of course meant the third row. The sun was by then in full command of the sky, and on the rain-polished pavements there was an avenue of light that pointed me down the street. I shuffled the cards again for more guidance. The nine of clubs.

I smiled. It was my favourite number. So that was where the girl lived. Number nine. Third row. I picked up my pace eager to see her again. When I arrived I knocked and smoothed down my hair. I stood for a long time and nothing happened. I knocked again.

The door opened a fraction, and a voice as soulful as a cello spoke. 'No point bothering me, I haven't got a TV, check my file if you must, not had one since 1974. No, thanks very much, not for me.'

'I haven't got one either,' I said.

The door opened wider. A slab-headed old man with a crown of white hair, looked out. 'You haven't?'

'Why bother?' I smiled. 'I get my answers elsewhere.'

'A clever man, that's for sure. Now, what can I be doing you for?'

I said I understood that the girl lived there and it was my firm belief that we were destined to talk again.

He shook his head. There were no girls there. Never had been, he said, girls didn't care for a free-thinking man like him.

'You've got to have more faith,' I said. 'When you believe, it happens.'

He shook his head. The door closed, not slammed, but closed nonetheless, and I felt something that I hadn't felt for many months. At first I couldn't place it, it was like tasting food with my eyes closed. I walked then, not because I had anywhere to go but because the street had stopped shining. It held less promise than it had before, and the strange sensation made me feel nervy, reminded me of a past when nervy was the norm. I pulled my coat tighter and marched on, wondering how I'd misread the cards.

I looked for a place to sit and shuffle my pack. At the end of the street there was a park. In the park a hill, upon which were mounted swings. I headed towards them until I came across a bundle of children. They had excited eyes and dirty knees. One stared at me, and I stared back, puffing my cheeks and making her giggle.

'Do you know a girl with a rainbow on her shoulder?' I asked.

'Rainbows are in the sky, silly.'

I sighed. And with that sigh came the feeling I'd run from, hid from, buried myself away from for as long as I could remember. Doubt, the greater destroyer, was back. I dropped to my knees and pushed my hands into my face, rubbed the palms up and down against my skin, and tried to black out the world.

'What are you doing? Have you lost something?'

I looked up and there she was, the rainbow girl, as beautiful as before.

'I lost you.'

She turned and walked up the hill to the swings. I followed behind, gripping the cards tight in my hand.

'Are you stalking me?' she said when I sat next to her.

'No, the cards sent me to the library and when I arrived I shuffled them to see which aisle I should sit in and there you were.'

She leant back and kicked out. Her legs swung into the sky. 'Are you for real, sheriff of love?'

'Listen,' I said, as she swung back and forth. 'I'm used to people not believing, but I have faith in the cards. They don't let me down like people. They tell me where to go to spread a little love.'

'You don't need cards to spread a little love, sheriff. I bet they didn't tell you I was hanging out in this park, did they?'

I looked at the crushed cigarette butts and sweet wrappers on the floor and said nothing.

'I didn't think so,' she said.

'Sometimes I read them wrong, that's all.'

'You should have more faith in yourself, cowboy. You know, if you didn't talk such a load of rubbish, I might let you buy me a drink later, but I presume you can't do that unless the cards say it's okay. I'm going home now, but I'll be in the Ship and Star later. I'm sure the cards will tell you where it is.' She jumped off the swing as smoothly as a gymnast.

'You'll be back,' I said.

She shrugged and walked down the hill. Of course I wanted to follow her. The thought of losing her again made my stomach twist and turn and my throat go dry, but I was sure she'd return. I watched her until she disappeared and then took the cards carefully in my hand and shuffled. The eight of hearts.

Eight o'clock then. Grinning, I waited on the swing, rocking back and forth, wrapping myself tighter and tighter in my coat.

The sun went down and still I stayed. The moon rose and I didn't shift an inch. Foxes sniffed around in the bushes. An owl sat like a judge in the tree. Only when the cold made my body feel as distant as a dream did I begin to wonder if I'd interpreted them wrong. I took out the pack and slowly began to shuffle. Then I thought of the rainbow girl sitting in the pub, and the fear of what I had to do hit me like a two-handed slap. Taking a deep breath and with trembling hands, I held the pack tight and tossed it as high as I could towards the stars. Jumping off the swing, I watched the cards flutter back to earth. Then, with them lying like litter in the dirt, I jumped off the swing and ran as fast as I could down the hill and into town.

Purged

I want to sweat out thoughts of Tamzin. That's why I'm in the gym six thirty every morning, while it still smells of lemon fresh from the Somalian girl's mop. Leave it to nature and your body gets soft like dough. You have to work it. You have to pump it. You have to crunch it. Too many men are like my dad. They let their bodies rot on drink and their minds on despair.

When I first saw the Somalian girl here, I thought of home. That would shock Dad. He'd spit and curse to hear that a girl like her made me think of Helsinki, but Finland's changed a lot since his day. He always said they were letting in too many foreigners. Not that he knew, stuck on the farm in the middle of nowhere with only Mum, me and the forest for company.

I remember the times when he'd go to the city for a tractor spare or fishing rod, and come back cussing with a frown as dark as midnight.

'Should never have joined that damned EU. Didn't spend the last fifty years paying the Russians off just so a lot of darkies could steal our jobs.'

'What about your cousin? He went to Sweden to get work,' my mum would say. 'Was he stealing jobs too?'

Dad would lean back in his chair, belly showing, and run one hand through grey hair that he still greased back. 'Your old woman talks a lot of shit sometimes, boy.' If I were near enough he'd clip me around the ear to emphasise the point. 'Don't you be taking after her, you hear me?'

I'd nod and his face, which Mum said was once as handsome as a tango singer's, would break into a grin.

Foreigners didn't want to work or learn the language. They treated their women like dirt, he said, hell, they couldn't even start a sauna. I wish he could've visited London to see what a city full of foreigners really looks like. Twice as many people here as in the whole of Suomi. Get on a bus and it feels like you're at the United Nations. That's why I came, for the people. To get away from the isolation that helped make Dad what he is. To feel part of the world instead of stuck on top, in a place nobody knows much about and cares for even less.

The Somalian girl's name is Amina. A pretty name for a pretty girl. Face is long like a horse's. Not in a bad way, but kind of noble, with eyes that hold you. She is different from Tamzin and watching her cleaning comes as a relief. She swishes the mop around the bench press like I'm not there. She has never spoken to me voluntarily. At first I thought it was the tattoos or the crew cut that scared her. Now I think she can sense something else.

Today, I stare at her as I do my crunches. I carry on till my gut goes numb. She's packing up her gear, dragging her bucket behind her as if it's a spoilt kid not wanting to go to school. She looks in one of the mirrors that cover the wall.

'What?' she says, catching my eye.

'Want to go out with me one day?'

'What?'

'You and me. I'll do the mopping for a week if you say yes.'

She laughs. 'You frown too much.'

I pull my vest up and look down at my abs. They shine with sweat. I clench my fists and punch them. The girl stops dragging her bucket to the store cupboard and stares.

I smile. 'It doesn't hurt. It's just a way of training.'

It's not. It's me trying to get rid of the feelings that refuse to go no matter how many crunches I do. It's me thinking of what happened to Tamzin.

Once I finish training, I take the Tube to Tamzin's house. She lives in one of those big terrace streets the English love so much. Road after road of houses exactly the same, with a garden no bigger than a bed in the front, and one not much bigger out the back.

The first time I visited, I'd asked her what was the point of such a small bit of dirt.

'It may just be a bit of dirt, but it's my bit of dirt,' she said. 'I can do what I please with it.'

'It's funny how people here care for scraps of land. It's what happens when so many people try to squeeze onto such a small island. In Finland, we have too much land and not enough people. The forests go on and on and on and they are almost totally empty.'

'Really? Fascinating,' she said, quickly checking the street before hurrying me inside. 'Now, chop, chop.'

At first, she was just like all the other English. She talked a lot, yet she never really listened. Even if I did speak her language and even if I was, as she claimed with a smile, 'the epitome of the Nordic hunk', I was still just another stupid foreigner.

Now, as I stare at her bright red front door, made even brighter by the early light, I remember how I found her on the kitchen floor. Half naked and battered, limbs sprawled like those of an elk that had just been shot. I turned her over. Her lip was split and her eye was swollen. Her black hair stuck to her forehead. Pink spit dribbled down her chin. I took a glass of water, held it to her lips.

She opened one eye.

'Where is he?' I said.

She grabbed a gulp of water. Her lipstick smeared the glass. 'He knows.'

'Where is he?' I repeated. The same question I used to ask my mum when I found her like that.

Tamzin shook her head. I lifted her up and buried my face in her hair. It smelt of marzipan and was so smooth I wanted to drape it over my face like a curtain. I got her dressed and took her back to my flat. Even in her state she seemed shocked how bare it was. A bed. A sofa. Table and chairs. An old photo of my mum baking *pulla*, held in place by a Finnish flag fridge magnet bought on a whim in the airport. I took her to my bed, stroked her hair and sung to her. It helped her sleep and it helped me control my rage.

In the morning, I found her hunched up on the sofa. The way she was trying to curl in on herself reminded me so much of my mum that I had to stop looking. I wondered as I studied the scars on my hands, if all beaten women looked like that. I didn't know what to say, so I asked if she wanted some breakfast.

'Come here.' She patted the sofa. 'I know I look a mess, but…'

I sat. 'You make my place feel as bright as a sunny day in winter.'

She put her fingers on my lips. 'You're a poet, you know.'

'Really?'

'Yeah, truly. You have a different way of thinking.'

'What, for a foreigner?'

'No, for a man.'

I held her to me, wishing we were alone in the forest. Wishing not for the first time that I hadn't moved to this country at all, with its people who treated you as dumb if you pronounced their words wrong, and its mixed-up weather and its claustrophobic cities.

'You know why I moved here?' I said.

'For the stunning women?'

'No. To get away from my dad and to live in a place totally different from the place that made him such an arsehole. I never want to be like him.'

She kissed my elbow. 'You're not.'

'I was,' I said, showing her the scars on my hands. 'Do you think you learn to be an arsehole or you inherit it?'

'Nature or nurture?'

'What?'

'I think it's a mixture.' She traced my scars with her fingernails. 'You're not an arsehole. I should know, I live with one.'

Later that morning she told me it was over. That she'd never meant for it to happen. That I was an adventure, a dare to herself, a luxury she could no longer afford. She stroked my face and said she was sorry, I was a lovely young boy and I should find myself a lovely young girl. Not a middle-aged troublemaker like her. I watched her leave from the window. She limped in her high heels, but she didn't look back. I felt the urge to break things rising in me like a sickness.

Only once has it taken hold of me since I've been here. Once in ten months. That's the longest I've been free of it since I left the army. I try to tell myself that I've done well. That once isn't bad. Still, it worries me that I still lost it so easily. It happened the third time Tamzin took me out, not counting the times she came to the café in Kensington where I wait tables and make overpriced sandwiches. We went to a club in Soho. It was in a converted cellar with red velvet on the wall and alcoves for getting intimate. A man, with a loud shirt and a louder mouth, asked her to dance. When she said no, he called her a slut. Perhaps it was the word, perhaps it was the sneer on his face, or perhaps I was already in love with her and I just didn't know it.

When I head butted him, his nose cracked. He staggered away holding his face, gasping like a man who'd stayed in the sauna for too long. Someone shouted. A bouncer grabbed my arm. I looked him in the eye and he asked me to leave. Outside, Tamzin wrapped her arm through mine as if we were promenading.

'Well, you're quite the action man, aren't you?' she said, her face flushed. 'I thought people only did things like that in those ghastly Hollywood films.'

I didn't say anything. Just looked at my hands. At the bitten nails. Later, in an all-white bar, she bought me fancy cocktails that tasted like melted ice pops. I didn't tell her that I don't drink anymore. I didn't want to lessen her sudden enthusiasm for me. Before we left, I went to the toilet, stuck my fingers down my throat and purged myself of the brightly coloured poison. The smell of vomit reminded me of mornings when I was a kid. Of my dad stumbling out of the bathroom, cursing with the stink of cigarettes and stale vodka wafting from him like foul aftershave.

Now, I stare at Tamzin's door, with my finger hovering over the bell. I want to tell her she can't just walk away, but I know she can because that is just what I did. Except I ran away. Ran away from the first girl I'd ever loved, so she didn't end up like my mum, or like Tamzin.

If I were at home now, I'd take a boat out onto the lake and stay there until the wind hurt my face. That's what I did when my dad used to beat me with a birch branch or slap me with the back of his hand or grab my hair and drag me out to the barn. That's what I did after I finished national service and my mum begged me to leave, telling me it would make her life easier.

'Why do you stay, Mum?' I asked, standing at the door with my rucksack.

'It's just his way. He loves me, really.'

You don't beat your wife out of love. You've got to have something wrong inside or you've got to hate the world outside. I wonder what it is for Tamzin's husband? I wonder what his excuse is? She told me once that teaching frustrated him. That he found the responsibility of nurturing young minds a strain. I think about that standing in front of his door. I think about those kids being taught by a man like my dad.

I walk to his school. Outside there are flocks of mothers. They all look the same. Hair messy. Eyes tired. Minds somewhere else. Like girls who grew up overnight. They stare at me. I see Tamzin's husband then. He's strolling through the car park, whistling.

I bounce on my toes. I feel a rush surge through me. I came to the city to lose this feeling. Now I know, as I breathe harder and harder, it will never go. It's me. It's what life made me. No matter whether I'm alone in the forest or in a city of ten million. If I have to live with it, best use it the right way. I clench my fists open and closed. Last time I felt it this strong was when I beat my dad, for the years of whacks and slaps, of punches and burns. For mine and for my mum's. Beat him till my knuckles bled.

Tamzin's husband doesn't see me until it's too late. He staggers at the first punch. The second knocks him to the floor. He yelps like a dog. I kick him over and over. Behind me the mothers scream. I carry on until he is quiet. Until my white trainers are red. When he is still, I walk away. I feel sick, yet purged.

Tomorrow I will ask the Somalian girl out again. And this time, with my frown gone, she will say yes.

All For Just Fifty Baht

Even though it's morning, the pavement outside Wat Ratchapradit is busy. In Bangkok, every hour is rush hour. Sinee crouches down next to an old woman sitting beside cages packed with sparrows, swallows and weavers. The birds bounce around, chittering and flapping and eyeing Sinee while she undoes her pink heels.

'Want to get rid of your sorrows, child? Only fifty baht for a swallow, seventy-five for a pair.'

The old woman flaps her hands. 'They fly so high they touch the heavens.'

'First I need to visit Buddha's house.'

Inside the temple she knows it will be cool and peaceful. It's beautiful, too, and difficult to find. Maybe her *farang* will get lost. Maybe she won't have to answer his question after all.

The old woman grins. 'Why not a bird first? One now, one after you speak with Lord Buddha. Think of all the good it will do for your karma. Give life to another creature, all for just fifty baht.'

Sinee smiles. Though the old woman talks like a street hustler, she reminds her of her grandmother. Sinee counts on her fingers. Nearly eight months since she left Chiang Mai. It feels longer.

'If Grandmother is to get better, we need money. There is no other choice,' her mother said. 'You must go south.'

She didn't mean to end up in Patpong, but the medicine was expensive and the wages were so much better there. The men were mostly okay and some, like her *farang*, were even friendly.

Tiptoeing down the steps, Sinee realises she has forgotten to remove her silver nail varnish. She feels exposed but carries on, head bowed towards the golden Buddha sitting cross-legged inside. Kneeling in front of him, she breathes in the sandalwood and jasmine until her throat tastes sweet. Two monks, boy apprentices

147

in mustard robes, sit at the side chanting soft words. Flowers, yellow roses and violet lotuses, lie at Buddha's feet. Some still beautiful, others wilted and old.

She tries to clear her mind but finds herself looking at the monks. Each wears a frown on his smooth, round face. They know what she is. Despite their glares, the temple calms her. She stares at the crinkled garlands. They make her think of herself in ten, twenty years. Only Buddha's smile comforts her and she realises that her *farang* often looks at her with the same expression. Feeling a little better, she lights a stick of incense.

She hears her *farang* before she sees him.

'Sinee, I am here! I am sorry I am so late. This has been so difficult to find. The tuk-tuk drivers speak even worse English than I. Do you want me to wait outside?'

She nearly nods, but he might touch her before he leaves and she doesn't want that. Not here. Not in front of the boy monks. She gets up, bows and goes to him.

'You look beautiful.' He dabs his head with a blue handkerchief. His yellow hair sticks to his scalp.

She tries to smile at him, feeling sorry that he has to lumber around the sopping city in his bloated body.

'I got you this.' He hands her a necklace with a jade S. 'I thought it would look pretty great with your eyes.'

She thanks him and slips it in her pocket. She can tell, by his hungry expression, he wants the answer now. 'I tell you, but not here.'

The monks' gazes flitter around her like startled moths. She ignores them. Her *farang* tries to take her hand in his damp paw but she pulls it away. Outside, the sun has cleared a path through the tin-coloured sky. There has been no monsoon today, but the world still smells like an old sponge. Sinee puts her shoes back on and listens to her *farang's* soft smoker's wheeze.

'I have not been around here before. Only that big old temple, Wat Pho. That one is pretty okay, but this I like more. This I could imagine in the forest at home.' He smiles. 'Like it has grown right out of the earth.'

He talks too much when he is nervous and too little when he is not. She wonders if she'll ever be able to handle the silences.

He nods at the old woman. 'They didn't have these birds in Wat Pho.'

'They aren't for tourists,' Sinee says.

He stares at Sinee as she walks towards the old woman and hands her a new note. 'Two swallows, please.'

The old woman snatches the money and reaches inside the nearest cage. With two quick jerks she grabs the birds and hands them over. Cupped in her hands, Sinee can feel their little hearts beating faster and faster.

'What will you do with them? Watch out for the beaks, beautiful.' He puts his arm around her. She flinches. 'Will you be happy in Helsinki without all this?'

Sinee holds the birds tighter, remembering the way her grandmother wheezed when she said goodbye. She pictures the flowers around Buddha, drained of their beauty, and the way the monks looked at her. After a deep breath, she kisses the swallows, whispers a few words and throws them as high as she can into the sky. When they are nothing more than swirling specks of black, she turns to her *farang* and answers his question.

Break a Brick

I draw my finger along the surface of my Akai reel-to-reel tape deck. Dust sticks to the tip. I do the same with my Pioneer quadraphonic sound system. More dust. I should've listened to my granddad. A pretty woman is a slovenly woman, Scott, he said, that's why your mum couldn't keep hold of your dad.

Well, they don't get much more slovenly than Pammy. She might look like Marianne Faithful, but the kitchen always smells of burnt toast and the bathroom is always littered with her tack. Lippy, bottles of empty perfume, Tampax.

I flick through my albums. Keen to listen to something raw and loud, I choose my latest purchase. *Bat Out Of Hell* by Meat Loaf. Just as the needle touches the vinyl, Snoopy strolls in holding a Rubik's Cube in one hand, his sailor Action Man in the other. I don't like to see him wandering around with dolls even if it's a plastic bloke with a scar, but he takes it everywhere. Even to the bog. His hair has grown longer since I've been away. Now at nine years old he manages to look like a cross between a hippy and a pageboy.

'Snoopy, get me a beer will you?'

'Dad, my name's not Snoopy.'

I laugh, because when he says this he looks more like Snoopy than ever. 'I know that. Just get me a beer.'

He opens his mouth, but instead of speaking, scampers into the kitchen. The music kicks in then. I let it ride over me as I pull open the top of my denim shirt and admire my tan. Snoopy comes running back in with a can of Carling, spilling froth on the new carpet.

'Watch what you're doing, mate!' I shout.

He flinches and walks more slowly. 'Mum says that instead of drinking beer, you should get the barbecue ready.'

I close my eyes and take a big swig. It tastes better than anything you can get hold of in Saudi. Even so, now Pammy's nagging, I'm already wishing I was back there, even if it means trying to teach a bunch of Arabs how to build a straight wall in a hundred degree heat.

'What time is it, Snoopy?'

He shrugs and sits cross-legged in front of the sound system, even though he knows he's not allowed there. I bet Pammy lets him touch it when I'm away. She pops her head out from the kitchen. She's frowning.

'Dave and Lynette will be here in half an hour. Don't you think you better pull your finger out and get changed?'

'I'm not changing.'

'You look like a cowboy.'

'Yee ha!' I shout, slapping my thigh.

Snoopy smiles and starts clack clacking his cube.

Besides Dave and his wife, Lynette, I've invited John and his new girlfriend, Nancy. Dave is an old mate, who I've known for donkey's years. His wife gets on with Pammy, so they always come over when I'm back. John I know from the pub. His girlfriend is buxom as a Page Three girl, with dimples and a glint in her eye. When she said she'd heard about my barbecue grub, I told her, you don't know what your missing till you've tried it.

'Ain't that the truth,' she said, grinning. 'I'd love a taste.'

The way she said it, the tip of her tongue poking out between her lips, I had to invite her.

Ours is a small town, a village really. It's one of the reasons I can't stand staying long. Too claustrophobic. Same people every day. Nothing much ever changes or happens, which is probably why my barbecues are so legendary. I brought the idea back with me from Oz, when I left the navy.

That's another reason why I work away. To make my life here more bearable. I've made the place as nice as I can with my Saudi work money. The sound system was my first purchase. I'd always wanted one, and it was great to be able to swagger into the shop and ask for the finest machine they had, peeling off the cash in notes. After that I bought Snoopy a pool table, but he never uses it. Too busy hiding in his room.

As for Pammy, she gets gold. Necklaces, chains, earrings, you name it. I get it from a bloke in Riyadh before I come home. Twenty-four carat, only the best. This time I got Snoopy a chain too.

'What do you think of that?' I asked, when he opened the package.

He held it in his thin hands, and licked it.

'What you doing? It ain't for eating!'

He looked up at me through that stupid fringe Pammy cuts for him. 'I just wanted to know what gold tastes like.'

He does stuff like that. It's Pammy's fault. Spoils him rotten. She says that I don't know how to be a dad because I never had one. She reckons I lacked a role model. Well, that's as may be, but when I'm at home I make sure he acts more like a boy should.

Today, I even let him help me set up the barbecue. He carries over the charcoal and the bits of wood, dropping them as he goes.

I shake my head. 'Where's the matches?'

He shrugs. 'Dunno.'

Next door's kids are kicking a ball about in their garden. One scores and runs around banging his chest and cheering at the sky. I spot Snoopy on his knees prodding some ants with a stick.

'They're in the fireplace, muppet,' I say, giving him a friendly clip round the ear.

He jumps up and runs off without a word. I had an open fireplace built for the winter. Snoopy loves it. Sits there looking at the flames like it's a TV or something. Pity he's not so enthusiastic about his football practice. The one time I watched him play, he touched the ball once. If I'm honest, I was bloody embarrassed. I sat in the car when the whistle went so nobody would know he was my kid. I never thought being a dad would be like that.

When Dave and Lynette arrive, I shout at Pammy to bring out some drinks. She appears with a big smile and a tray. She's done something fancy to her hair, and has gone Cleopatra crazy with the eyeliner. It works, though, and I suddenly feel all nostalgic for the good times before we got married. Like the night I saved her from getting bundled in a mosh pit at a Kinks gig and she gave me a slap for ruining her view.

'Do you want a drink, darling?' she says, all sweetness and light.

When I nod, she gives me a fresh can and a full-on kiss. For a second, I feel guilty about the French airhostess I met in Riyadh. But then she goes and kisses Dave and Pammy and I realise she's just putting on a show.

By the time John and Nancy turn up, the sausages are sizzling and Pammy has put the Stones on the sound system. Nancy looks fantastic. She has these cute little arse-hugging shorts on, and a T-shirt that's perfect for showcasing her tits. When she kisses my cheek, I take a quick sniff of her perfume.

'Blimey, you smell better than my bangers,' I say, pushing the sausages around the grill.

'I should hope so,' she says, all mock offended.

The sun has gone down and we've cracked open the Southern Comfort when Dave asks me to break a brick for them. I've been waiting for this all evening. It happens at every barbecue and I always go through the same routine. First I pretend I haven't heard and try and change the subject.

Dave starts shouting, 'Come on, show Nancy and John what you're made of.'

'No, I can't be bothered tonight.'

'It's bullshit, I reckon,' John says, challenging me.

'I can assure you it's not,' I say, winking at Snoopy.

They all start chanting. 'Break a brick. Break a brick. Break a brick!' Even Pammy, who thinks I'm stupid doing it.

I hold up my hand. 'Okay, but only because you've been such great guests.'

They cheer and clap.

I nod at Snoopy and tell him to go and get a brick, while I pick up a couple of breezeblocks.

'Can I watch, Dad?'

'I thought you didn't like karate,' I say, remembering the time I took him to join the club and he hid in the toilets pretending to have the gut rot.

He doesn't say anything, just looks at his fingernails like they're the most important things in the world.

'You can watch me do one, then you get to bed. You hear?'

He nods and runs off.

I clear a space in the centre of the patio and set up the breezeblock and place the brick in between. I look at the crowd. Dave's got this manic grin on his face. Lynette is holding her hand to her mouth. Pammy is telling John something with this I'm-clued-up expression. And Nancy is leaning forward, staring at my every move. I catch her eye and she giggles.

'Be careful,' she says.

And I nod, all serious, even though I've done this a hundred times before. I take off my flip-flops and roll up my flares. Nobody says a word. The only noise is the stereo. The Who playing 'My Generation'. I lift my foot up as high as I can above the brick. The higher it is, the faster it goes, the more force it makes. Speed, focus and power. The holy trinity of breaking. I breathe deep. Scream my breath out and blast my foot through the brick.

Someone, Nancy I think, squeals. The two halves of the brick clunk to the floor. Snoopy starts clapping in a way only kids can. Everyone else joins in.

'Fuck!' John says. 'How do you do that?'

'Years of training,' I say, and it's true. I'd be a black belt by now if it wasn't for Pammy and the boy.

'That was brilliant!' Nancy says.

I take a bow.

Pammy comes over and puts her arm around me. She nibbles

157

my ear, and kisses me. I can smell the vodka on her breath. I call Snoopy over and mess with his hair, and for a few seconds it feels good, like we're a normal family or something. Then Snoopy says he feels sick and Pammy lets go of me and starts cooing at him like he's a bloody baby. I look at them and think about how my mum used to lock me under the stairs if I made a fuss about anything.

It's well past midnight when I meet Nancy on the landing. She's wobbling all over the place, but still in better shape than the rest of them. I lean against the wall, but she makes no move to go past me. Instead, she runs a hand through her hair and asks how my foot feels.

'Fine thanks. How does yours feel?'

'My what?' she says, and pushes her chest out.

It's pretty obvious what she wants. I think about it for maybe half a second, before deciding I'd be a fool to turn her down. Opportunity only knocks once and all that.

'Your softest parts,' I say.

She takes my hand and cups it on her tit. 'How about that?'

'Works for me.'

She grabs me then and practically slams me against the wall. Before I can tell her to be quiet, she is grinding herself against me and sticking her tongue down my throat like it's the last kiss she'll ever get. I look over her shoulder and see that Snoopy's door is wide open. Nothing's moving in his room, so I let her carry on.

I've got my hand on her arse and she's whispering dirty in my ear, when we hear someone messing around with the sound system. She lets go and wipes her mouth. We both hold our breath. The music changes and somebody shouts her name.

She grins. 'Another time maybe,' she says and totters down the stairs.

I watch her go before lurching into the bathroom. I look at myself in the mirror and shake my head. You're too bloody smooth to move, I say to my reflection, even though I'm already starting to feel a bit of an arsehole. I splash some water over my face and take a piss. Before I go back downstairs, I poke my head around the door of Snoopy's room. I can just make him out laying still, arms above his head like he's sunbathing.

I smile. Silly bugger. 'Goodnight, mate,' I whisper and make my way back to the patio.

Next morning my head's clanging like a pile of pans and my mouth feels like a dustbin. Pammy's dribbling into her pillow, her mascara smeared over her face like a bruise. I stare at her until I hear a noise downstairs. Banging. Metal on brick.

The banging stops by the time I get to the landing, replaced by a sizzling, hissing sound. I walk down slow because of my head. In the living room I find Snoopy sitting in front of the fireplace. There are still embers burning from the fire I made last night, and stuck in the embers is the poker. The boy's in his Spider-Man pyjamas, all hunched up over something. I'm just about to bawl at him when I see him pull the poker out of the fire. There's another sizzle and a wisp of black smoke flies above his head. A smell like burning tyres fills the room.

'What the fuck are you doing?'

I see his body shudder and for a second I think he going to hurl it at me.

'Snoopy!'

I grab his shoulder and spin him round. His face is flushed from the fire and his eyes are red. In his hand, he's holding his navy Action Man. It's still wearing its hat and it's still got its blue and white uniform on. But where its mouth and nose were there's now a gaping hole of melted plastic.

'Bloody hell! What have you done that for?'

He looks up at me through his fringe and his mouth quivers, but he doesn't say a word. I ask him again, but he just carries on staring. Then I see that his fists are clenched and he's breathing hard. And I realise that the look he's giving isn't his scared one and his lips aren't wobbling out of fear or shame or embarrassment. I realise that he's angry, angrier than I've ever known him.

'I saw,' he says.

'Saw what?'

'You kissing that lady.'

I put my hands on my head and slump in my chair. We sit in silence for a few minutes. I feel like I've been punched in the gut. I wonder why he hasn't blabbed to his mum.

'Listen, Snoopy, it was just a game. I had too much to drink.'

'My name's not Snoopy,' he says, staring at his charred doll.

'I'm sorry, Dylan.'

He doesn't say anything, just sits there.

After a while, I pat the arm of my chair. 'Come here, mate. You keep this our secret and I swear on my life I'll never do it again.'

He sniffs and looks at his chewed nails for a while, before clambering onto the armchair. I pull Abba out of Pammy's section of records, and hand the vinyl to Dylan.

'Here you go. You can put it on if you want. For your mum.'

He doesn't say anything, just holds the record in his hand like it's made of crystal. Then, looking through his fringe, he bites his lip and smiles.

Skin Against Skin

Edgar ambles down the high street, past smiling couples, bellowing families and teenagers bristling with energy. It feels as if everyone is going too fast, and only he is moving at the right speed. He tugs at Nelson's lead. His dog's nose is glued to the pavement and every thirty seconds he cocks his leg. Edgar leaves him to it, knowing when he's sniffing and pissing he's happier than a virgin cabin boy in a brothel. It's then that he spots Percy with Edna May, his Edna May, promenading down the pavement opposite.

'God in heaven! See that, Nelson? See that old bastard across the road with Edna?'

The dog looks up at him with his one decent eye.

'I can't bloody believe he'd do such a thing. Not to me. Not after all these years.'

Nelson carries on lapping a chocolate wrapper like nothing has happened. Edgar yanks his lead, then apologises when the dog yelps. By the time they get back to the bungalow, Edgar's heart is pounding, just like the doctor said it shouldn't.

In the living room, first thing he does is grab his bottle of Johnnie Walker. Another thing the doctor said he shouldn't do. One swig warms him up, but not till the third hits his belly does he feel any better. He wanders over to the mantelpiece and picks up his wedding photo. Dust puffs off it and there is Edna May, all showered in confetti.

'She was a good girl then, Nelson. A looker, too. Who'd have thought after all this time she'd do the dirty on me with him next door. Three hundred and fifty dog years, he's been my mate. Spent nine year at sea with him. Just you and Gavin now. Only ones I can trust.'

Edgar coughs, and tips his head back. He can feel himself chocking up. It happens more often these days, but he holds his head back and the tears stay where they belong. Nelson runs out into the garden and Edgar follows him outside. It's a fine day. Too fine. The garden's looking bright. Flowers doing well. The birds are bantering and bees getting busy. It's hard to believe that a day like this could have kicked him in his gut. He starts feeling sorry for himself, and then he sees Percy's carpet-smooth lawn. And that's when it hits him. He's not taking Percy dilly dallying with his other half lying down.

'The way he mows that bloody grass you'd think he was a groundsman at Wimbledon.'

At the bottom of Percy's garden there's a battered armchair. It's leaning again a shed, stuffing is bursting from it and its leather is all cracked. Edgar picks up Nelson and throws him over the fence, then hauls himself over. He's got two voices in his head. One, which always sounds like his old Captain, is getting arsey. It tells him it isn't worth it and he should reconsider. But the other voice, the one which sounds more like him, is louder. Make the bastard pay it says.

He cracks his knuckles and looks at the armchair more closely. Must have been a grand piece of furniture once, but it's nothing but a wreck now. He scrambles behind it and, with a deep breath, pushes it towards Percy's house. The lawn starts peeling away in great big chunks. He ignores the pain spiking his bad leg, and carries on until he's right outside Percy's back door. Then, with a sigh, he sits down. He feels tired and the lawn all churned up doesn't make him feel as good as he'd hoped; still the leather feels nice against his arm.

'Damn, Nelson, I miss skin against skin. That's what I miss most. I was with Percy the first night I learnt the pleasure of it. Singapore Palace, me and the lovely Lilly Lee. I'm showing you how to be man, she said. And God in heaven she did, too.'

Nelson whines and that's when he sees Gavin leaning over the fence, staring.

'Granddad, what the heck you doing there?' He jumps over.

'Shit! What you done to Uncle Percy's lawn. He'll go ballistic!'

'He betrayed my trust, Gavin. Simple as that.'

Gavin puts his arms round Edgar. 'Let's get you indoors. I'll have a talk with Percy. Tell him you got a bit confused, then you can have a word with him.'

Edgar pushes him off. 'Don't bloody well patronise me, lad. The only talking I'll do with him will be with these.'

He holds up his fists. The tattoos, can still be made out, but where there were once beautiful ocean-blue swallows, there's now nothing but black smudges.

'What you going on about?' Gavin says.

'I saw him with your grandmother. Bold as bloody brass.'

Gavin shakes his head. 'So what? You haven't been married since before I was born.'

'What?'

Gavin repeats what he thought Edgar thought he said.

Edgar looks at the lawn and massages his temples. Sometimes getting everything straight in his head is like trying to juggle jelly. Things that make sense one minute, suddenly don't seem so certain. 'No matter,' he shouts louder than he means to. 'He betrayed my trust. He's my bunkmate and he shouldn't be seen out with my wife. Even if we aren't married any more.'

'Come back into the house, Granddad, and I'll give you a game of draughts.'

Edgar carries on staring at the torn turf, thinking his old Captain might have been right all the time. 'If I'm a vandal it's only because I've been provoked. You understand that lad don't you? Now, I've only got one mate left and when I die I want you to look after him.'

'Granddad, you aren't dying.'

'When Nelson kicks it, I want him buried with me.'

Gavin shrugs. 'I'll see what I can do.'

Edgar is about to tell him he'll do better than that when the old fellow in question starts barking. The backdoor opens and out strolls Percy, smiling like a matinee idol. Edgar feels a sharp twinge in his chest and wonders if his heart has finally called it a day.

Percy stops right in front of him. 'Bloody hell! What've you done to my lawn? Have you been drinking for breakfast again?'

'Keep away from my kin, understand?'

'What's got your goat?'

Edgar lunges at him then. 'How could you do it? I saw you with her, not an hour past.'

'Who?'

'Edna, that's who!'

'You silly sod…'

Edgar doesn't let him finish. The punch isn't as hard as ones he's thrown in the past, nowhere near, but Percy takes it right on the nose. Blood drizzles over his shirt.

Gavin grabs him. 'Stop it, Granddad! He's just been helping her, that's all.'

Edgar is shaking. He looks at Percy, who's trying to speak through his fingers. The words are all clogged up. 'Her back's gone. Can't carry a thing.'

'What's he going on about?' Edgar ask Gavin. 'Why didn't she ask me?'

Gavin shrugs. 'You never go and see her, do you?'

It comes back to Edgar then, a great gush of memories. Him leaving her when he came back from sea and heard talk of her dancing with some fella. Him punching the fella, so hard he broke his knuckle. Him finding out later, too much later, that it was nothing. Just a birthday dance. He looks at the faint scars on his knuckles and wonders how many years past that was. Percy is staring at him. He's a good mate to take care of her like that, Edgar thinks.

'I'm sorry, pal. My head's not what it used to be.'

'Your head was never up to much,' Percy mumbles.

'I'll help you do it up again.' Edgar nods at the lawn.

'That's not good enough. You can bloody well go see Edna May too.'

'What?'

'You heard. I'll look a right state tomorrow and I'm not doing any errands with a face like a pig's arse. You'll have to help her.'

Edgar looks at Gavin again, but he avoids his eye. 'I don't think that's a good idea.'

Percy wipes blood off his nose. 'You've ruined my garden and smashed up my face, so if you don't want to take the risk, take your scraggy dog and piss off home.'

Edgar stares at him and at the lawn. They both look a proper mess. He wishes he'd never taken Nelson out. Wishes he just stayed at home and done a bit of weeding in the sun. Half a bottle of Johnnie Walker is sitting on the table in his living room. I'm too old for making up, he thinks, I should just go and polish that off. Get the day over and done with. But then he sees the look in Gavin's eyes.

He stares up at the sky, puts his chest out and stands up straight. He might lack sense, but he's never lacked courage. That's what his captain used to say.

'Be a good lad, and get your Uncle Percy some tissue and a glass of beer, will you, son,' he says, waving Gavin over. 'And pick up Nelson's lead too. It looks like me and him have got a visit to make.'

All Because

In 1968, Cadbury introduced the Milk Tray Man to the world. For nearly four decades, this tough action hero overcame a vast array of obstacles to deliver Milk Tray chocolates to beautiful ladies.

He was the first person I ever truly admired. That unabashed Romeo moving amongst the shadows was everything that I, a pimpled stick of a boy, could only ever dream of being. No wonder then that I so relished watching his daring deeds. Sitting in front of the TV, hugging my boney knees, I'd chew my knuckle as he dangled from helicopters or leapt from hurtling trains. No obstacle was ever too great to stop him delivering his precious cargo to the woman he loved.

My enthusiasm for him would most likely have withered and died, like so many childish things, had my parents not been so suddenly taken from me. Even now, years later, I can still see Mrs Mower's expression as she called me to the front of the class, and I can still smell the rosewater on her floral blouse when she hugged me to her chest. A heady mix of emotions washed over me, yet it was only the tiniest taster of what was to follow when, after an eternity, she let me go and led me to the headmaster's office to hear the news.

A terrible accident. He was very, very sorry. Try to be brave, he said. The rest of his words were lost as Mrs Mower sobbed and drew me once more to her immense bosom. And that was where I dealt with the news, wedged between her breasts. I don't know how long I stayed there, but when she let go, I wished I might go back and stay in their warm embrace forever.

As an orphan, the gentleman in black became ever more important in my life, the father I no longer had. I imagined my mother, her beautiful eyes looking down upon me with delight as I planned a way of delivering joy to the women of the world. Look at my son, isn't he a wonderful and sweet boy, so kind and brave, she'd say to the audience of angels, who'd flutter their wings and nod in agreement.

The older I got, the more determined I became to spread happiness. The love I could no longer give her, I would give to other women. I was fourteen when I made my first delivery. A box tucked under my arm, I sneaked into the girls' dorm, heart pounding so loud I was sure that at any second the sleepers would stir and scream to the heavens. With a shaking hand, I slipped the package onto the bedside table of Anna Goodwin, pausing only for a second to admire the soft curve of her lips and the delicate slope of her nose. The pleasure I felt on returning to my bed was only surpassed the next day when news spread of the mysterious Milk Tray, which had so magically appeared beside her.

Even if I'd known what fate would await me, I wouldn't have changed the course of my life. For without these adventures, my time on this earth would have been one of unbroken tedium. To some, it might seem strange that so much joy can be gained from the secret delivery of a box of chocolates. But let us not forget that chocolate, so readily available these days to every Tom, Dick or Harry, was in ancient times a gift from the gods.

Straight from paradise it came, so the Aztecs said. Carried by Quetzalcóatl himself as he travelled to earth on a beam of light. By eating it, you were blessed with wisdom and power. Though I'm no god, and I doubt my mouth-watering gifts endowed their recipients with these talents, I like to think that when the ladies awoke they felt something akin to wonderment.

This belief has carried me through the bleakest of days. It is what I repeated to the police officers who cuffed me like some common criminal, and what I told Detective Sergeant Heaton when he questioned me. It still pains me to remember the way he sneered at my answer.

But I do not ask for pity. I'm merely a product of a system that has treated me as an inconvenience since the very day my parents passed away. As I gaze over the skyline of a town that houses more than a million unhappy souls, I wonder why our society so vilifies a person whose genuine, heartfelt desire is to spread joy amongst his fellow human beings.

Now that parole has taken that opportunity from me, I have no choice but to leave the country of my birth. I do not for an instant blame Miss Brook for misunderstanding my intentions when finding me in her bedroom. I blame myself for being so casual in my preparation and so clumsy in my execution. Such sloppiness is unforgivable to one with so many years of success, so many missions completed and so many boxes of cheer left behind as magically as coins from a tooth fairy. Carelessness is no doubt a symptom of arrogance and it seems I fell pray to that very vice.

So now it must end. I have made all the preparations. My bag is packed and my bills paid. I have dressed for the journey in my uniform of black roll neck and trousers, but before I close my door forever I will indulge myself and enjoy a final Milk Tray fancy. Like any sane man, I have a soft spot for soft centres. My most enduring love affair, though, is with the Strawberry Kiss. It is not just its gooey sweetness, but the fond memories it provokes of my darling mother's habit of always saving it till last.

Relishing this final taste, I think ahead to my new life in warmer climes. The only thing that tinges me with sadness is that when my quest begins anew, I will have to use a different box of chocolates. It will not be the same. Everybody knows that ladies love Milk Tray. But, although the magic they'll feel upon awakening will not be as great, even the smallest dash of magic is surely better than no magic at all.

Acknowledgements

Firstly, thanks to all the editors of the publications who said yes to many of these stories. 'One Bright Moment' originally appeared in *The Best of Every Day Fiction 2008*; 'The Wrong Bus Girl' in *Prick of the Spindle*; 'Buy Ma Biscuits or Kiss Ma Fish' in *Riptide* and on BBC Radio; 'The Cost of Advertising' in *The Remarkable Everyday*; 'Lola's Chair' in *Pangea: An Anthology of Stories from Around the Globe*; 'Estella and the Gringo' in *Voice from the Planet;* 'Burnt' in *Message in the Bottle and Other Stories*; 'The Grounding of Tiffany Hope' in *The Bristol Short Story Prize Anthology* and on BBC Radio; 'All For Just Fifty Baht' in *Southword*; 'Break a Brick' in *Not About Vampires: An Anthology of New Fiction Concerning Everything Else.*

The act of writing is by necessity a lonely business. Happily, everything else to do with writing is not. Many people have helped with this book, some without even realising it. I'd like to especially thank Alex Keegan for setting me on the right path, Vanessa Gebbie for her constant warm encouragement, and everyone who critiqued my work in Bootcamp, Writewords, Fiction Workhouse and Fiction Forge. Thanks also to Tom Vowler for his kind words and Adam Monaghan for his cool photos. Huge thanks to Ian Daley, Isabel Galan and everyone at Route Publishing for being incredibly patient and working magic on my manuscript. I'd also like to thank my family. My mum and dad, Sally and Paul, brothers, Oliver and Harry, and sister Gemma for inspiring me. My step dad, Peter, for helping choose the cover. My parents in law, Riitta and Pekka, for their enthusiasm. My children, Lotte and Eliot for simply being fantastic. And finally, Anna Maria, my amazing wife for being the best critic, editor and muse any man could ask for.

Photo: Adam Monaghan

Since leaving the English county of Suffolk, Joel Willans has lived in London, Vancouver, Helsinki and an Andean village in the Peruvian department of Apurímac. Currently, he lives in the Finnish countryside, in a converted hospital sauna, with his wife and two children. A partner at the communications agency, Ink Tank, his prize-winning stories have been broadcast on BBC radio and published in dozens of magazines and anthologies worldwide.

For further information on this book,
and for Route's full book programme
please visit:

www.route-online.com